MW01135522

The Citadel

2019

"Stories from Los Angeles"

Featuring the work of LACC students, faculty, and the surrounding community.

Cover design: "Shadows Over the Sunset City" *(m. acrylic paint on watercolor paper)* **by Adrian Garcia**

Published by:

The Citadel Board of Directors – Nadia Elahi, Dr. Danielle Muller, Jeffrey Nishimura, Daniel Ruiz, and Flavia Tamayo

https://www.lacitycollege.edu/Academic-Departments/English-ESL/The-Citadel

Editors: Judith Dancoff, Dr. Genevieve Patthey, and Daniel Ruiz

Editor-in-Chief: Flavia Tamayo

The work within these pages is representative of the voices of Los Angeles City College, but the writers' words are their own and are, therefore, not officially endorsed by the college itself, or the Los Angeles Community College District.

Second Edition: October 2019

This edition was made possible by the generous support of the Los Angeles City College Foundation.

http://www.laccfoundation.org/

ISBN 13: 9781088888360

Table of Contents:

Editor's Note

I once asked one of my students in a creative writing class why she writes, and without missing a beat, she responded, "Because I have to. It's not a choice." What you have before you are a myriad of voices who have brought their stories here, especially for you, because they must speak, and they must be heard. So, it is with great joy and pride that the LACC English/ESL Department and the editors bring to you the 2019 edition of *The Citadel* and "The Stories from Los Angeles."

The Citadel has been published at Los Angeles City College since the 1960s and provides a space for students and the community to share their voices. We are a college and a community at-large made up of a rich, diverse fabric that is our strength. This strength in diversity is reflected in the stories, poetry and art that our students and community offer you within the pages of this journal. *The Citadel* provides an outlet and a space for our students and community to share in the human experience, and we hope it is an outlet that you will continue to support and find worthwhile.

The collection of voices within this journal reflects those of students, faculty, established writers, students learning English as a second language and inmates from the California State Prison, Los Angeles County (LAC) in Lancaster. Although many of our contributors come from different walks of life, their stories, poetry and artwork speak to the human condition – life's struggles and triumphs – that we all share. The stories and poetry range from a tale about a mystical flying muumuu and the realities of racism to a sublime drive through the streets of Downtown Los Angeles and childhood love.

You will hear voices and see artwork that reflect love, pain, happiness, despair and redemption.

In addition to our students and surrounding community members, we have also included a section that speaks to the lives of the incarcerated. Thank you to fellow co-editor, Professor Judith Dancoff, for helping to make this portion of the journal possible. I would also like to extend a special thank you to Marlene McCurtis, a teaching artist who works with the Los Angeles County inmates, and Susie Tanner, founder of The TheatreWorkers Project, who submitted the stories and poetry from the inmates included in this journal. We hope that you find their stories as heart-wrenching and uplifting as we did.

Something new that we have included within the second edition of *The Citadel* is artwork. Thank you to Professor Alexandra Wiesenfeld, Chair of Visual and Media Arts, for bringing us such amazing artistic pieces by our very own LACC students! Thank you to the students who allowed us to reprint their work for all to enjoy.

Of course, *The Citadel* would not be possible without the support of the LACC Foundation which has generously funded this project for the past two years. The LACC Foundation does a tremendous amount of work for our students, and we hope to continue our collaboration with them throughout the years. Finally, thank you for taking the time to open this book and read the treasures within it. We hope you enjoy it, and we hope to have your continued support for years to come.

Gratefully,
Flavia Tamayo
Editor-in-Chief

"Broken"
(*m. black-ink on water color paper*)
by Richard Johnson

Lola
by Caresse Fernandez

A sliver of what was left of the waning moon reflected upon the water. Through years of drought, rain was rare in Los Angeles and the conditions over the past month were a complete anomaly. For almost the entirety of October, rain poured relentlessly night and day. Climatologists were still trying to come up with explanations for the strange occurrence, but Michelle comforted herself as she remembered what her Lola would say. *Ayun nanaman si Anitan Tabu.* "Anitan Tabu is at it again." The Filipino goddess of wind and rain was usually more likely to be airing out her grievances out in the islands, but she could very well have brought them over across the Pacific just like Lola Marcy had brought over Michelle's parents right before Michelle was born.

Whatever the reason may be, she was glad that the skies had finally cleared and allowed for her to get back to her nightly runs around the lake at Echo Park. These runs were her reprieve from the long days at the office. She was happy to help her patients deal with their issues, but this was her chance to let them go and make space to sift through her own. Much like the lake had reached its capacity for water, the backlog of problems her body had endured due to her thoughts started to build up, and they needed to be expelled.

By millennial standards, Michelle was in a great place for a woman her age. Fresh into her thirties, she was a successful therapist going on her second year of practice. She was living on her own, almost completely debt-free, and had a good close-knit group of friends. She did struggle with her on-again, but mostly off-again, relationship with her girlfriend, but that wasn't high on her priority list. Equipped with a charming smile, dotted with her almond eyes, she was content with the regular rushes her Instagram account could procure for her through a flurry of likes. She was pretty content with her life.

Unfortunately, her life wasn't truly hers. Both of her parents had been unemployed at the start of the financial crisis in 2008, and as older immigrants, it wasn't easy to bounce back and find another job. Since Michelle started working retail in high school, and through odd jobs in college, over half of her and her brother's paychecks went into making sure that her parents were okay. This stood to be true ten years later, and it didn't help that her parents were divorced and living under the same roof out of necessity. Michelle and her brother, Renato, had become the parents giving out allowances and regulating tantrums.

It had been two weeks since she had heard from her brother. After finding out that their mother had used his credit card to buy a new mattress without asking, he had reached his threshold and told her that he was done playing caretaker. Michelle stayed silent as her brother chewed her ear off over the phone about how their parents didn't deserve the kind of support they had been giving them. Her silence only angered him more, and before he hung up for the last time, he tersely declared: "You only let them take over your life because you're too afraid to live out your own."

Michelle had given her all to run off that last sentence. She muttered it to herself, over and over again, and each time the words sank heavy into her bones. She thought that this run would be her way of shaking off all the built-up tension, but it was clear that this first lap was purely for processing. It all needed to move in her before it could move out.

Things had started to lighten up during her second lap once she started focusing on her breathing. She started to find her stride as each step became more spirited in place of the leaden pace she had begun with. Michelle had finally started to feel like herself again—less lost in her head and more present in her body. That was when it all began.

Out from behind one of the few L.A. palm trees yet to be ridden by disease, an olive duster dress with a yellow floral print had started to trail behind her. It hesitated for a moment before deciding to glide along next to her. Michelle had seen it in her periphery but didn't think anything of it until it started to frantically flail its sleeves around to call her attention.

"Am I really this tired already? It's only been a mile!" she thought to herself as she continued along the path.

She looked around to see if anyone else had noticed the dress floating alongside her. It appeared to be imperceptible to the other runners and bystanders (a likely result of their preoccupations with their respective Fitbits and paramours). Slowing her pace, she took a better look at the dress. It was older; you didn't need to have a vintage aficionado to tell you that. At first glance, you could tell that it had experienced more than someone twice Michelle's age, including an attack by moths to the left thigh. Michelle surmised that it was at least seventy or eighty years old. She couldn't figure out why, but it felt familiar to her—and that distant familiarity kept her attention.

Suddenly, reality set in, and Michelle processed the objective truth: She was interacting with a flying muumuu. In complete disbelief, Michelle shook her head and told herself that this was what she got for breaking her routine. She blamed the rain and wanted to air out her own grievances with Anitan Tabu.

The dress floated effortlessly in front of her, blocking her from continuing her route. She reached out to touch the garment, and it pulled back to dodge the attempt. It turned away from the lake, due south towards Temple Street, and prompted her to follow.

Michelle, determined not to have her overdue personal therapy session disrupted by a ghost of a garment, turned around and started running in the opposite direction. The persistent pajama would not have it, and as soon as it had made its way in front of her, it held its position, forcing her to run into it, face first. The dress disoriented her and turned her back around. It prompted her to follow again, this time with more urgency.

Michelle sighed, realizing that her resolve was not as strong as she had thought. As she ran to tail the authoritative dress, she decided, "I am definitely looking into getting a therapist of my own again tomorrow."

Uncle Martha
by Gregory Raygoza

Uncle Martha wiped the tables, mopped the floor, and counted the money, stealing some for herself. She took a little every day, sometimes more, sometimes less, a few dollars here and a few dollars there, like love notes tucked discreetly into her jean pockets. Not a greedy woman, or even desperate, she just wanted more than food and rent. There was never enough money to save, and time had narrowed her future from a horizon to a needle's eye. Saving for the future seemed like a luxury afforded to other people, people she didn't know. She'd likely never retire: Working until death was part of her family's legacy. Her grandfather had died of a heart attack while feeding grease into a machine that kept on pumping without him. They found him slumped over with black grease and urine puddled around his lace-up work boots.

Martha sprayed and wiped the gold-vein mirrors, scraping off a bit of hardened muck with a plastic fork, avoiding eye contact with her reflection. She'd been looking more like her grandfather as she reached the age of his final year: white hair on her knuckles, flapping jowls, inflamed joints, and a snow-white crew cut. Beyond a few key details, her failing memory had muted the sound of his voice and dimmed the exact proportions of his face. A scooped nose and ornery eyes like an ostrich were all that she could recall. Her eyes were friendlier than his, less intense, but with the same bushy brows. Her grandfather was never one for pictures. "Pictures are for beauties," he'd say slapping a camera away from his face, "and ain't a goddamn beauty in this house." Uncle Martha hated pictures too.

She carried only one picture in her wallet, her old bullmastiff, Martha Junior, who'd been left at the pound for his ugliness by his previous owners. Martha fell in love the second she saw him: a chewed up right ear, a cleft palate, and wide-set eyes. He looked permanently distressed, but he was generally inclined to good spirits. He never seemed worried about life, which fueled Martha's optimism. Heart problems and other bodily imbalances chased him his entire life, but it was finally cancer that got him. Uncle Martha had to put him down. A good friend was gone. He had never cared how much she drank or if she didn't pay bills on time. He came to her when she laughed and came to her when she cried. Through the good times and bad, he loved her the same. She missed him more than she missed most people, living or dead.

She gave up on cleaning the mirror. It was as clean as it would ever be. The bar was calm and tidy now. It was mostly quiet except for the muffled sounds of laughter and flirtation from the boys lingering outside. Martha cut the lights and stepped out into the night, locking the door behind her.

"Uncle Martha!" a sloppy Joan Crawford called out. "Uncle Martha! I'm out of bus fare and I'm hungry!" He pouted and teetered on his heels. Earlier that night, he'd crammed his feet into a pair of sling backs, busting the strap. They were a bad replica of a good shoe, not built to last, and certainly not built for excess capacity. By the end of the night, they'd end up left behind on the roadside.

"Didn't you make any tips tonight?" Martha asked.

"Bitch, you saw my act! I was lucky I made it out of there alive! You got a few bits of cash you can spare?" he begged playfully.

Martha pinched the money from her pocket and handed it over.

Joan Crawford counted it carefully, twice, mouthing the numbers suspiciously. "*All* of it?" he asked.

"Sure thing, baby doll. I saw your act and I thought it was great."

"*Awww*, you flatter me so."

"Actually," Martha hesitated, "the act was lousy, but you can keep the money anyway."

Crawford blew her a kiss and stumbled backwards, his dress tearing a bit at each side. Uncle Martha walked on.

The usual stragglers lined the sidewalks, grown men dressed like horny children, looking for someone to go home with. A few of them paired up or huddled in threes, telling secrets to each other that no one else cared to hear. Others screamed and laughed, saying vicious things about one another, things that were true but easily forgiven in their gaiety. The further Martha walked, the less and less she heard them, until her work was far behind her and all was finally quiet.

A quarter mile along and she crossed the old Spanish bridge that led home. With its pillar-guardrails and crumbing aediculae, it was an imitation of the ancient past, a stately presentation as if to suggest that it had always been there and that it would remain so forever. Electric lanterns cast shadows, revealing cracks and twists, like a tired old spine about to snap, taking the body down with it. Water rushed gently beneath, flowing much higher than usual. The decade-long drought was finally over. A decade-long drought with brown mountains, yellow lawns, and uncontrollable summer fires that wrapped a hot, gray blanket over the city. A whole lot of nothing happened in those ten years. There were a lot of pizza and beer, and plenty of women, some sweet and some cruel. Uncle Martha had been good to them all, an expert at anticipating needs. Women assumed, from Martha's size and demeanor, that she'd be their mama bear, there to hold them, protect them, and guide them through life. Few of them ever assumed that it was Martha that needed guidance and protection. She had a private sadness about her that inevitably exhausted the ears of her lovers. Young women wanted fun. Old women wanted stability. Martha was stretched thin between the two extremes. With each woman who left her, there was something new to drink over and something new to cry about. It was then that she missed her old dog the most.

Of all the women she'd known, Candice was the one she loved best. Candice, with her sepia face, flat, wide, and true. She regarded Martha's body so lovingly, intensely, almost with a violent lust in her stare. Martha didn't like it at first, self-conscious of her nakedness. Her body was all low-hanging and soft curves, the weight of herself draped in supple folds all around her. Candice seized her with a force greater than her own strength. She was about half of Martha's size, a boyish chest, thin, with an empty sagging flesh at her midsection. She was short and loud, like a small dog, scampering up and down the streets, chasing life without reason and taking food off everyone's plate. She was good to Martha, took care of her sexually. Martha didn't expect much extra, except for the occasional back rub and a hand grazing the stubble on the nape of her scalp. Candice was pleased to please her.

Martha and Candice walked together, doing anything that didn't cost money. Hand in hand, they compensated for the disparagement in their size, Martha leaning slightly down to one side. "How's it going down there?" she'd joke, waving down to Candice. Candice waved up and smiled like a happy child. Martha recalled many good days and not so many bad ones.

Up on the bridge, with the cold coming in, Martha remembered them walking on a blistering day. Candice wore a pair of plaid boxer shorts and a rib knit tank. Martha wore her favorite Hawaiian shirt and cargo shorts, what she called her *vacation dad* look. They didn't bother with catching any shade or beating the heat. There'd been hotter days, much worse. They'd seen it all. They kept on walking. Their path took them along a stretch of sidewalk vendors, huddled brown people, walking up and down the line, among miscellaneous goods: battered toys, piles of rusted saws, broken guitars, fresh fruit, cheap fur jackets, and framed photographs of Jesus as far as the eye could see. Candice rummaged through dollar bins, trying on tarnished rings and Martha tried on men's blazers. Martha looked at herself in a nearby mirror, straightening her back, not accustomed to the structure of tailored clothes. She imagined herself in an office, opening letters and signing checks, with a picture of Candice on her desk. She thought about all the things that she could do if some great hurricane of cash blew her way.

"If I had a million dollars," she said, "I'd buy a million more!"

Candice looked at her cheerfully and joined in, "I'd buy a nice little ranch with chickens and pigs." She paused to admire a brassy ring on her finger. "I miss pigs. I'm through with people. I need to be around animals for a while." She palmed the ring discreetly, and they continued down the street.

"I don't mind people so much," Martha contemplated for a second and continued, "You know, if I had money, I'd ride around in a golden Cadillac handing out free tacos to everyone. I've never seen someone sad with a free taco in their hand."

"I'd buy the dress Patsy Cline was buried in."

"I'd buy a shark skin suit and a box of Cuban cigars."

"I'd buy a little baby monkey!" Candice exclaimed. "A little baby monkey that I can love like a daughter. I'd put little baby monkey dresses with a great big bow on her head!"

"I tell you what I wouldn't do even if I had all the money in the world," Martha declared, "pay my bills!"

They went on like this for another mile, bouncing dreams back and forth, their hands gripping tighter as the streets grew more crowded. They walked and walked in the blissful heat, then took a sweaty, naked nap in Martha's bed, crossing their wet limbs over each other, and kissing whatever bit of flesh came their way. The ceiling fan kept a steady and comforting beat. Their breathing synched, and they fell in and out of sleep together, opening their eyes and smiling, then falling asleep some more. Candice stroked Martha's cheek with a slow and steady pace, watching her face submit to rest, drooling and snoring and completely relaxed. Nothing was between them, no clothes, no crowd of people, no rusted saws, or cheap fur jackets. It was just the two of those aging women, naked and at ease, without anyone to please but each other.

Martha tried to remember the rest of that day, but the details were lost. There was probably pizza.

There was probably beer. Martha probably went to work that night and served Candice free well drinks until the end of her shift. And they probably ended up back in bed, tangled together. But Martha couldn't exactly remember.

Alone on the bridge, Martha looked out into the dark, down into the moonlit river, and asked, "How's it going down there?" But no one answered back.

The wind blew in stronger and a fierce cold came from between the shadowy hills, a cold wind that grazed her body like a straight razor. She'd forgotten her fleece jacket at the bar. *Oh well,* she thought. *Too damn far now.* It'd be there tomorrow night, waiting for her on the back of a chair. Hopefully, by then, it wouldn't be so cold.

The Party
by Lena Becerra Bartilotti

"Hi mom. I have no reception in the park, so I just drove out to call and make sure we are all set for the party," I said on the morning of my son Matthew's sixth birthday party.

"Okay, sweetie. I have everything you asked me to bring, and I'll be there at nine-thirty. Are you sure you don't need me there sooner?"

"Thanks, but I've got it. I have all the decorations and the piñata. Only one of us has to be here early to claim the picnic tables anyway, and that gives me plenty of time to set up. Dad's bringing the ice and ice chest. Todd will bring the pizzas, the water, and the birthday boy at ten o'clock!" I said.

"The birthday boy! I'm so excited. I can't believe he's six!" she exclaimed.

"I can't either," I said.

The weather is always warm in early August and becomes insufferably hot by the end of the month. Still, in 2014, I thought I'd roll the dice and throw my son's birthday party in the park in late August. I had been a single mom for three years and had been stuck with the complete bill for birthday parties every year. Saving money by throwing the party in the park rather than shelling out for the hosted venues was alluring.

I arrived at the cement picnic benches, painted a terra cotta color, at Bronson Canyon, a shaded section of Griffith Park nestled at the foot of a hill. There were a few large oaks, silk oaks, and eucalyptus trees to aid our effort to stay cool from 10am to 12pm. Griffith Park is a 4,310-acre area of the eastern Santa Monica Mountains, 3,015 acres of which were donated by Griffith J. Griffith in 1896. Griffith J. Griffith would later go on to shoot his wife in the head while vacationing in Santa Monica, disfiguring but not killing her. The irony never eludes me that I've spent so many joyful hikes with my son in a park whose donor had a dark streak. But in the early 1920s, the Union Rock Company created an open pit mine to excavate rock to pave the city's streets, leaving behind a perfect cave. The television series *Batman* used the cave to film the Batmobile driving out of the Batcave in the 1960s, and so you have the perfect attraction for a six-year-old's birthday party.

The weather was still pleasant, a little chilly even, at 7:00am. I had a tumbler full of strong coffee in the center console of my blue 2007 Toyota Corolla that still had the faint scent of the previous owner's dog on hot days. I loved my car for being reliable and inexpensive. I hated my car for being a symbol of how I had not risen above the point of counting pennies in the four years since taking a full-time professional job in health insurance. I had sidelined my dream to go back to graduate school full-time in order to be financially stable. Instead, I was neither an academic nor financially stable. My car was my daily reminder that I hadn't made it, and years had passed. I turned the rearview mirror toward me, took a quick look at the pronounced bags under my eyes from lack of sleep, took a long drink from my tumbler, and started to unload my car.

I was the only person in this part of the park. I carefully taped down the blue, silver and green plastic tablecloths over the picnic tables covered in bird poop. I strung twine between trees to hang the homemade blue, white, silver, and green tissue pompoms I had spent weeks making with friends. I carefully strung the blue, green, and silver streamers along the sides of the tables and between the trees to make sure they were twisted just right. I would not have a repeat of Matthew's fourth birthday when my friend Sophie and Matthew made the streamers look more like TP-ing than decorations. I then blew up the balloons and taped them to corners of the tables and around the trees. I opened the soft set of soccer goals for the kids to play with and set the soccer ball about halfway between them. I took a look around. It was just like I imagined when I planned it. I sat down.

Matthew's birthday always lands in the first week after the school year begins. We learned this in kindergarten and decided to give birthday party invitations to his whole class on the first day and, to our surprise, most people showed up! We decided to keep the tradition and invite the whole class again now in first grade. My mom arrived with the fruit and vegetable platters I asked her to bring, and she helped me fill the piñata with candy until, one by one, children showed up with parents and some siblings, too. My ex, Todd, arrived at 10:05am with Matthew.

I greeted Matthew excitedly, "Hi sweetie!! Happy birthday!!" I turned to Todd, "Hi Todd. Where's the pizza and water?"

"I have to go to Costco right now and get it," he blurted abruptly.

"Why didn't you get it before and just bring it with you?" I asked condescendingly.

"Because they don't open until 10am," Todd snapped back.

"Oh, I didn't realize...then why not order it from another place?" I asked.

"Look, I pre-ordered it. I just have to go pick it up. This is way cheaper than any other place, and it tastes better. I'll be back in thirty minutes," he said.

"What about the water?" I asked in a panic.

"I'm going to grab it while I'm there. Sitting here talking to you about it isn't going to make it happen faster. I'll be back," and he left.

I could feel the adrenaline course through my veins, and my hands quivered a little. Why didn't I just handle this part myself? I would have paid the extra money to order from Domino's or something. But he agreed to provide the pizza for the party, so the decision was his. I felt a tightness in my chest. I took a deep breath and turned back to my guests with a smile.

The kids saw the soccer ball and knew just what to do. They started playing with no teams, no rules, no goalies, just running and kicking and trying to get the ball into any goal. Parents from the school gave each other familiar hellos and slowly settled into casual conversation.

"So, Lena, how's everything going at work? I heard you got a new position—a promotion, right?" asked John, a good-looking actor in his early forties with an even better-looking wife.

"It's going well! Thanks for asking. The new position is way more interesting. It sets me up better for advancement, and I really needed the raise. But it is a lot more stressful, too," I answered. I hate that I tend to overshare when I'm nervous, and I want people to like me.

"You got a new position *and* you're working on a graduate degree, right? Is it related to your job?" asked Anthony, an older dad who made his career building charter schools and has photos of himself with the Clintons framed in his home.

"Oh, I am and no it's not related at all," I laughed. Then reading the blank stares on their faces, I explained,

"My dream is to be a professor at a Research 1 university, but I kind of put it off. So, when Matthew was one, I went for a master's degree in Chicano Studies, but realized that wasn't *the thing*, so now I'm in a philosophy MA program. But I don't have to finish, because the professor who is supervising me just said my project is ready for Ph.D. applications this fall. So, I'll be applying in the next few months!"

"So, do you want a career in health insurance or an academic career?" Anthony asked the question John was too polite to ask.

"Either, I guess. I mean, I don't know what I want. It's my dream to be a professor and writing research papers is what I love doing! But, if I don't get accepted anywhere, then I want to advance as much as possible in this company and have a really good quality of life." I hadn't really thought it through. That was obvious.

I had started the MA in Chicano Studies when Matthew was one. By the time he was two, I realized I didn't make enough money to support him teaching part-time and got hired in a full-time project management position at a health insurance company. By the time he was three, I was divorced and had to raise him on my salary alone, so I started looking for advancement opportunities. I was working in school to lay down the foundation for an academic career and at the office for a professional career. I couldn't seem to let go of either of these two parallel tracks, and this awkward conversation was becoming more common among my colleagues, family, friends, and classmates.

"Well, it sounds like you're doing well either way. Good for you," John said in his usual polite manner.

"Yeah, but you're going to have make a decision at some point. It doesn't make sense to split your efforts like that, and you're a single mom," Anthony never minced his words. He and his wife, Linda, were both like that, and I liked that about them. They occasionally had me over, and we'd chat while Matthew played with their son, Jacob.

My cheeks felt flushed even though it hadn't gotten significantly warmer. I started to sweat. "I will. One of these career tracks will either take off or end, right? I don't have to decide right now," I said in an unsuccessful attempt to end the conversation.

"You can't work full-time or even part-time in an academic doctorate program. So, it would just be the student stipend, right?" Anthony said.

"I know, and I'm applying mostly on the east coast, so I'd have to quit my job no matter what if I get accepted. But people do it. I don't know exactly how, but other single moms have done it," I stuttered.

"Yeah, they don't usually leave good paying jobs to do it," Anthony said knowingly.

John's daughter, Valerie, came over and asked, "Is there any water?"

"Well, Matthew's dad went to get it and," looking at my phone I said, "he should be back in about ten minutes. I'm sorry, but can you hold out for ten minutes?"

"I'm really thirsty," she protested.

"Val, you'll be fine. Ten minutes. You can handle it," John said to alleviate her panic. "She'll be fine," he said to alleviate mine.

The kids began to lose interest in the soccer ball, so I said, "Let's walk up to the Batcave!" I turned toward the parents and said, "The water will be here by the time we get back, so it'll be perfect!"

The group of about twenty boys and girls were raring to go. I was surprised they were so excited to see a cave, but it worked for me. Matthew was ecstatic to lead the way with so many friends in tow.

"I'll hang back and keep an eye on everything," Anthony said.

"We've been meaning to bring Val here. We just haven't yet. So, we were pretty excited when we saw this on the invite," John said.

As we walked up the hill, I gravitated toward my mom. Other parents clumped together, and I watched Matthew reel in excitement surrounded by his pack of friends. Suddenly, Matthew was down on the ground and friends were hopelessly trying to aid him. I ran over, weaving my way through the sea of kids.

"Ouch! Ouch!" he repeated in pain.

"It's in his sock!" one kid yelled.

I started to panic, and everything started to blur, but if there's one thing motherhood has taught me, it's that I don't get to be weak. Not even for a second. I tuned out the chaos of screaming kids and focused on Matthew, searching for the source of the pain. And then I found it – a sandbur in his sock. This small spiky ball grows on weeds in dry areas. It measures only about a centimeter in diameter, but it looks larger when it's stuck in the delicate skin of a six-year-old's ankle. His calves had just recently started to change shape, elongating and displaying ever so slightly more muscle tone as the baby fat began to fade. I slowly pulled out the sandbur when I realized there were more – many more in both of his socks, some in his shorts, and in his shirt. I calmly removed each one and then joked, "What did you do, roll around in the bushes?" His large, round, brown eyes brightened, and he cracked a smile with his cheeks that still had some baby fat left, even if they were starting to slim. He stuck out his arms for a hug, thanked me and ran off again with his pack.

"He'll live to see another day!" I laughed to the parents who were as worried as I was by the kids' reactions.

The walk to the cave was longer than I remembered and completely exposed to the sun, so the cool of the cave was a welcomed relief. It's a short walk through the cave, so the kids decided to just hang out in the cave yelling at the top of their lungs and running top speed in every direction for no reason. I tried to keep my eye on every kid in the dark tunnel. Matthew made his way over to me, "Come on, mom! Scream with me!" He followed his own request with an ear-piercing screech, tugging on my hand until I joined him. One on one, I'd join him in a second! I'm the one who taught him to yell in tunnels for fun. But in front of the other parents, I was a little self-conscious they'd think I was childish.

I took photos of the kids jumping and cheering at the mouth of the cave, and when the novelty wore off, we made our way back to the shaded meadow with the picnic benches.

"Todd's still not here," my mom reported what I had already discerned.

John approached me timidly, "Hey, no pressure but is there any water, yet?"

"It should have been here, already. I'm so sorry," I replied.

"No worries. None at all," he said kindly and walked away.

I went over to the ice chest my dad had brought, full of ice but no water. Anthony approached me and said, "Hey, Gelson's is just down the street. I'm going to dash over there and grab some water for everyone."

"No, no! I should. I was going to leave when Todd got here to grab the ice cream anyway," I protested.

"You're the host, you should stay. I'll grab the ice cream, too. It's easy," he said reading the guilt in my eyes. As I started to pull cash out of my purse he insisted, "Absolutely not! This is easy. No big deal. I'll be right back."

Matthew came running over, "Mom! We are going to have teams! Watch us!" Dave, the screenwriter dad, who always volunteers at the school and whose emergency-room-doctor wife never can, was forming teams and refereeing a soccer game. Kids were arguing calls and keeping score. The heated match came to a complete stop as soon as Anthony arrived with the water and ice cream, though just long enough to consume them, and the game resumed as abruptly as it had stopped. Matthew kept an eye on me to make sure I was tracking the game.

"That was a near disaster," I said to my mom.

"The water? Yes, but you have a great group of parents, and you've built great relationships with everyone," she said.

"Yeah, I mean Matthew's been in three seasons of sports now with these kids and has known some since preschool. So, we've spent a lot of time together."

As I looked around the meadow at the party, I saw more than just a group of people enjoying a kid's soccer game. I saw solid adults Matthew had come to admire, who had coached Matthew's sports teams and had become invested in Matthew's growth. I saw really good kids being guided by parents with similar values as mine. I saw people consistently offering to help each other out, pitch in, volunteer, and build a healthy and nurturing environment for kids – people who were totally invested in their families, not just going through a routine and getting by. I saw good role models for how to be healthy, responsible, and caring adults. I liked being with them, and I liked being one of them. Because we all live within one mile of the school, we'd see each other at the grocery store, at the movie theater, and at the park. I saw stability, continuity...community.

I felt pressure in my chest and even though I didn't want to cry at Matthew's birthday party, a couple of tears defied me and rolled down my cheeks. I turned to my mom, holding my posture straight, and my chin up so Matthew wouldn't notice I was crying.

"Mom, I can't go to a doctorate program."

"I know," she said.

"You knew?" more tears escaped. She quickly passed me a napkin. "But you babysat all these years for me to attend classes and write my thesis. You read through draft after draft, and then learned my whole new interest in philosophy to talk through ideas with me."

"It's your passion," she said.

"I keep saying I haven't decided, but there *is* no decision. He's six. He has friends and community. He's planted roots. I can't give him all of that by myself especially if..."

"MOM! I made a goal!!!" Matthew exclaimed across the grass.

"I saw!!! Great job!!" I lied with an enthusiastic smile. He went back to his game. I turned to my mom, "especially if I'm overwhelmed with work like I have been this last year. I mean, he was five and now he's six, and I missed it. I missed that whole year."

"No, you didn't. He doesn't feel like you did. You two spend so much quality time...."

"I know what I missed," I cut her off. "You see what I did, but I know what I missed. I wasn't fully present because I was so busy and I kept thinking things would just ease up, but I missed it. His whole fifth year."

"Okay, well that's not true. You took him to Ireland and New York City, and skateboarding, and hiking, and to the trampoline park," she said. "And you *could* make it work if you chose to pursue an academic career."

"No. I've been lying to myself," I said looking down. "I looked at the student health plans. They don't include dependents. I took the project management job specifically to get him good health insurance. The stipend is less than half my salary and student family housing is the same cost as my current rent. I wouldn't even have the money to buy him health insurance." I looked her in the eye again, "I could give him the best childhood if I stay right where I am. I'm gambling with his childhood if I don't."

She looked at me with eyes that knew from experience what it meant to wait too long to commit to your dreams.

Then Todd pulled up.

"Pizza!!!" Matthew screamed then the others echoed, and they ran toward Todd's car. I helped unload.

"The party is more than halfway over! What took you so long?" I asked when the kids were out of earshot.

"That place was a nightmare! I pre-ordered, but you still have to stand in line outside, plus the line inside for the water was already like twenty carts deep. And I couldn't call you because you have no reception here. We really shouldn't have his party in a place with no reception again," he snapped.

"You missed more than half of his birthday party!"

"I know! It sucked. I'm really upset! But look, my dad's in town this weekend, so can I take him the rest of the weekend?" he asked. Todd's dad, who lived in Idaho, had never come to Los Angeles to visit before, and he'd recently been diagnosed with Parkinson's.

Even though I wanted the weekend with Matthew, I replied, "Yeah, that's fine."

After some pizza, more water, a piñata and some sweaty, exhausted good-byes, it was done. Only my mom and I remained finishing the last of the clean-up.

"It was a great party, Lena," my mom said, "everyone had a great time and said so."

"Thanks, mom. I felt like a complete failure with the water situation."

"It was fine. Everyone was fine," she said.

"Mom, what will I do now? Just report to an office every day and nothing else?" a tear fell as I finished my question.

With complete confidence she said, "You will find a way to use your talents. There are more ways to impact the world than being a professor." We sat in silence for a moment. Then said our goodbyes.

I got in my car, took a quick glance in the rearview mirror at the puffiness in my eyes from crying, looked down at my tumbler and decided to drink the cold coffee. I thought, "Maybe if I get another promotion, I'll be able to get a new car."

Too Nice
by Mareshah "MJ" Jackson

"Full of themselves."

It's a common saying — often from men — and usually in reference to the women who ignore their gratuitous questions, who don't stop for a "Hey," while on their way to work, or who avoid eye contact in passing. On this bumpy train ride, while speaking to a man who had previously bypassed ten empty seats to sit next to me and wave his hand in front of my face, I hear the phrase for the umpteenth time, but in a different way.

"You must not be from here."

"Nah, I'm from Virginia."

"I knew it! I could tell you weren't from L.A.; you're too nice. Girls here are too full of themselves."

He says it like those other girls should be ashamed, like I should be proud in comparison. As he offers his name and continues his inquiry into how long I've had my locks, the left side of my brain mulls over the idea that this rare instance of patience with a stranger on my part somehow translates into my allegiance to a certain quadrant of the country, or a certain level of humanity. And then, what was that about other girls being "full" of themselves? I consider what's more appealing: being full of oneself, or being an empty vessel, always open to being filled by another person's questions, opinions, and energy.

I'm still smiling — "Thanks! But no, I don't make house calls to do hair" — but my stop can't come fast enough. It's been a long day, and it's about to be a longer commute home. My face is tired. The inevitable appeal to exchange phone numbers thankfully comes right as the train doors open to familiar red and yellow tiles; I deny him entry to my life via my phone screen and escape without having to see if his feelings are hurt or answer any manipulative questions. I leave the already nameless man behind at Hollywood and Western, but the question of being empty or full follows me off the Red Line, onto the 207, and into my studio.

Stupid, right? I mean, what kind of question is that — of course I'd rather be full. All the best things are full: bellies, bank accounts, halves of glasses. But something about his tone, and the tone of folks before him, gets to me. I've always been that girl. Chill, passive, quick to laugh — never considered to be full of herself. Most of the time I'm okay with that, but lately I've been feeling an undeniable exhaustion after sustained interactions that serve only to enthuse another party. A need to wear a heavy, grinning shell wherever I go. An emptiness.

Thinking about those "other girls," the ones who stay full of their own energy, I get a little indignant. In a way I feel protective of them, though I have a feeling these full women under the L.A. sun could not care less about the opinions of an entitled stranger on a train. These women who I've never met, who could also be from Virginia, or Ohio, or the I.E. for all I know — they don't care about my opinions, either. They'll be fine.

I pick at the options the way a little girl might pick at flower petals: *Empty, or empty not? Full, or full not?*

The same two questions run silently through my brain on a marquee while I accept the delivery charge and add a 25% tip to my order on Postmates; while I pray I tipped enough so that the next person with a colorful name isn't held accountable; while I chew my spaghetti as I scroll through my ex's Instagram; while I wait for my roommate to exit the bathroom, guts bubbling away; while I shower with body wash that dries my skin (it was a birthday gift); while I forgo sleep for just a few more minutes of Twitter, then Instagram; then Facebook — although I hate Facebook; then back to Instagram. Yes, my ex's page. Somewhere in my brain, there's a joke floating around about how the "me" time I'd been craving all day has been completely devoted to everyone else, but I'm too tired to form the words. I keep scrolling.

The next morning, any grogginess I feel from a lack of sleep is overridden by the rant I laid on some guy in my dreams. I'm so enthralled with the memory—who knew the dream version of me was such a badass?!— that I rush to stand in front of the mirror and rehearse the parts I remember:

"Oh, L.A. girls are stuck up?" I reach up for the head wrap I slept in and whip it off, dramatically. Immediately I regret it — I looked regal with the scarf, now I just look goofy — but I keep it going, because recalled dreams are so rare.

I glare at myself above the sink. "You tell me —" I pause, not able to take myself seriously. This would be so much better if I'd had my coffee. I lean forward to rinse the sleep from my face and try to channel the slinkiness of Cardi B in the "Red Barz" video.

"How about we discuss what it's like living in a city that's so damn expensive you don't have anything left to smile about after you leave your third contracted job of the day, hm?" My face in the mirror begins to morph into an amalgamation of faces that have demanded my time or space in the past few years. Most are faces of strangers, avatars of my imagination run wild. But every now and then, a countenance I recognize well surfaces to the top. I'm setting my own cuckoo radar off, so I pull the medicine cabinet open, grab my toothbrush. I continue the monologue in my head, though — it's not crazy if your mouth stays closed, right?

As I get ready for the day, I relish my mental motion picture debut. As I'm laying a verbal attack on this stranger I've never met, but met a thousand times before, he stays silent, cowed by all the points I'm throwing his way like softballs:

Zing! "You asked me a 'yes' or 'no' question, I gave you a 'yes' or 'no' answer. I don't understand why you're following me around like a lost dog."

Zing! "Here's a pro-tip, dude: headphones mean I'm not trying to hear you. Scrolling through my phone means I'm not trying to see you. Both mean, 'leave me the hell alone.'"

Zing! "Why are you asking if I have a man? I already said I'm not interested."

Zing! "Oh, now you think I'm rude? Maybe if I wasn't between healthcare plans for the third time this year, I'd be able to get the medicine I need to have a bitch-free conversation with you, sir!"

By the time I'm dressed, made up, and on my way to the train, I'm laughing at myself. The daydreams in my head have gotten impossibly corny, a clear symptom of a childhood absorbed in 20th century teenage redemption movies. Yet, as I reach the entrance to the Red Line station, a small part of me still isn't laughing; it feels heavy. In my daydreams I felt so free, and now I'm back on the escalator descending into a space with very real social demands.

At the landing, as if on auto pilot, my eyes lower at the same time my steps quicken. I quickly scan for a comparatively empty spot on the platform that I can fill, and once I find it, take up residence. I pull the top half of my heavy hair into a knot, keeping my earbuds as visible as possible. There's no music on, but I like the illusion, even if they make my ears itch. I scroll Instagram — not my ex's page (this time) — and realize that less than six hours have passed since I fell asleep with my phone in my hand last night. In two minutes, I've already seen every new post and story update that's taken place since I've last checked, and I'm incredibly bored. Still, I continue to scroll because I need something to do with my hands and my eyes.

"Hey."

Damn. Where did this one come from?

"Psst. Excuse me."

Doesn't he see my headphones? I take a long blink and turn around to look up at the man — *it's always a man, isn't it?* — standing above me. I'm irritated and upset with myself for being so irritated. Girl, chill. Maybe he needs help finding his stop. I know as well as anybody how easy it is to confuse the Blue Line with the Ex —

"I saw you from over there. What's your name?"

"My name? I'm sorry, do you need help with something?"

"I'm just trying to get to know you. I saw you standing over here, alone. A pretty girl like you shouldn't have to be anywhere by herself." He smiles, and he'd probably be handsome if he wasn't so wrong. If I'm not surrounded by the white noise of social norms and imaginary judgments, I'm standing in the shadow of some guy, just like this one, saying whatever I think will appease him most. I'm never alone.

I bet only women who are full of themselves get that luxury.

I give him a stiff nod as I respond, "Oh, okay. I'm fine."

"Oh, I don't doubt!" He follows this with another smile, even as his eyes flicker downwards. I wonder if he knows I notice him scanning me, or if he even cares. He's standing too close.

Against my better logic and what the girl of my dreams would've done, I smile in return. It's 7 a.m., I want to separate myself from everything for just a moment before work, I do *not* feel like pretending I'm interested in a random guy who, up 'til now, has only seen me from behind... but I muster up the energy and smile even though it feels like my whole head is splitting apart in the dry morning air. Talk about a habit that's hard to break. People think social media has made us addicted to cultivating ourselves online, but I feel like I've been cultivating myself in person for ages.

What would happen if, for once, the person I was most worried about pleasing was myself?

A few long seconds have passed, and I'm just now realizing I've been glazed over, staring this guy in the eyes with this dumb smile on my face. His smile's still there, albeit weaker, and he's waiting for me to thank him for gracing me with his presence and keeping me company, or maybe for interrupting whatever playlist I *could* have been listening to, for all intents and purposes. He's waiting for me to move to the side and empty myself so he can plug himself in, even if only for a few minutes on the platform. I get a glimpse at the arrival times: two minutes left. I pray he's not also going to Union Station.

For a second, my grin drops, and I consider dropping my protective armor with it. I could open up – let him know how frustrating it is for another adult to purposefully ignore all the hints I'm throwing his way. How irritating it is that the social cues I work so hard to cultivate never bring me peace.

"So...you gotta number? Instagram?"

As I get ready to open my mouth, the guy's eyebrow raises, and he pushes his chin forward in unmistakable impatience. Something about his attitude wakes me up; I could open up, or I could preserve myself. Just this once. The protective armor comes back up, but it feels lighter. With a grin on my face I slowly, deliberately, put my left headphone back in my ear. It works; the exact moment he catches my ironic rejection is apparent in the fall of his face. My thoughts run down a list of scenarios as the screaming train comes closer. Maybe he'll push me off the platform or call me a bitch for all the women and children to hear as a warning for their own future interactions. Maybe he'll just be openly embarrassed and cause my face to heat up in solidarity while bystanders shake their heads at me, disappointed in the state of relationships "these days." My calmness in the face of his annoyance and all the possibilities it holds surprises me. I've always thought of myself as someone who would never do anything to put my physical safety or my reputation at risk. But here I am, risking.

Per usual, my personal thoughts are way more dramatic than the real thing.

After a couple of offended blinks, he swats his hand at the air between us. A gust of wind blows between us as the train flies through, right on time.

"Fucking L.A. girls, man," he mumbles, stalking off. "You're all so full of yourselves."

Red lights blink as the train doors welcome me inside. I'm alone, full of nothing but myself. I'd take this over the alternative any day.

On Getting Woke
by Sharon Kyle

The first day of school, my sister and I began the short walk from our grandparents' house to the high school in our new neighborhood. The new digs were fine, a little cramped, but this was a temporary arrangement. All else aside, it was nice being with my grandparents. We hadn't seen them as much in the eight years since they'd moved from their apartment in the Bronx, bound for California. Now the four of us—my mother, sister, six-year-old brother and I—temporarily shared a bedroom in their small bungalow while Mommy figured out what to do next.

What started out as a summer vacation had quickly evolved into something with entirely different possibilities. A month into our summer with Granny and Grandpa, Mom had been offered a job by a family friend. When she accepted it, a new world opened to her.

Now that the summer was ending, she needed to decide. Should she return to our father in New York or try to make a go of it on her own with the kids in California. She could end their relationship and start anew on the west coast. She was young enough, just 35—and a young 35 at that. Most people thought we were sisters.

Her marriage to my father had been a disaster. Married just a few months out of high school, it hadn't worked from the get-go. Maybe it would be better for us all if she just called it a day. We hung in the balance waiting to know our fate. In the meantime, we kids would have to find a way to adjust to La-La Land—at least for now.

Our new neighborhood was pristine, says the Bronx native who, up until then, hadn't travelled much. As my sister and I headed toward the school, my mind drifted back to when we'd first visited Granny and Grandpa all those years ago.

"This is a black neighborhood?" I asked. Truth is, it was 1965. Where else could they have lived? Grandpa took us on a drive, touring Long Beach, Compton and Watts. I'd always heard Watts compared to the Bronx or Harlem, but the contrast couldn't have been more striking. Rundown tenements, abandoned buildings, and vacant lots were all standard fare in the Bronx. Watts, on the other hand, consisted of single-family homes with grassy front yards. The people living there had their own private backyards. This was not at all what I'd imagined.

Fast forward eight years and my sister and I walked past dozens of neatly manicured lawns—the palm trees that lined the sidewalks gently swayed in the breeze as we made our way through this strange kind of "hood." I liked to think of our new neighborhood as "Hood California Style," but it really looked more like a postcard. Another perfectly sunny day in California. Did it ever rain in this place?

I don't know what it was about L.A., but something seemed to be amiss, and it wasn't just the lack of rain. I couldn't put my finger on it. I just know that I always sensed a kind of hollowness—an artificialness. As picture perfect as the neighborhoods looked, there was something that just didn't line up. Maybe it was that the sidewalks were empty, no pedestrians, really no people, not even in the parks, not even walking dogs—as if we were on a Hollywood movie lot complete with facades. Compared to New York, it looked like a ghost town.

My sister and I continued walking down the streets that had no people. We could see the main entrance of the school.

By the time we walked through its huge doors and found the front office, I was beginning to feel a bit anxious. But being the big sister, I'd mastered the ability to keep my cool and act like an adult. My focus shifted to the task at hand: look out for my sister and get us both enrolled. I was prepared and had no doubt that I'd be able to handle whatever we encountered as the "new kids." But, prepared or not, I felt a deep sense of relief when I was informed that we were not going to be able to get into school that day.

As soon as the administrator heard me say that we were new to the state, she told us that we were in the wrong place. We'd have to enroll at Lakewood High School, a full hour away by bus. That meant we'd have to wait another day and get my mother involved. We had no idea where this Lakewood school was or how to get there. My mother had a car and would have to take off from work, from a job she had just started.

I guessed the reason was that the school was overcrowded. Having to attend a school in another city meant that my sister and I would have to get up a little earlier to catch a bus and arrive home a little later. But aside from the extra transit time, I didn't think this arrangement would be too problematic. It wasn't as if we would be leaving friends behind. We were going to have to make new friends anyway. I figured we'd just have to do it in Lakewood instead of Long Beach. No big deal—or so I thought.

After a few phone calls arranging for our enrollment and getting directions to Lakewood, the three of us were on our way, this time with my mother in tow.

We walked into the administration office and inquired about enrolling. We were all ushered into the principal's office. How strange was this?!

I wondered if the principal had one-on-one meetings with all transfer students. I'd never been called into the principal's office. Where I came from, the principal didn't get involved in school transfers. The principal at Lakewood High was nice enough. Most of our conversation consisted of small talk. I kept wondering if he didn't have something better to do. But towards the end of our "visit," he posed a question that gave me pause.

He told us that Lakewood High School had a student body of approximately 3,000 and that all except for two students were white. He wanted to know if we thought we'd have a problem with that. Did I hear a tone in his voice that seemed to suggest that he was asking if WE were going to be a problem? I wasn't sure. But the mere fact that he was laying this out in this manner suggested to me that maybe there might be a problem.

Just three months before this meeting, I was attending a New York City high school where the student body was about 60% white and 40% people of color. In some classes, I was the only black student. I couldn't imagine the principal asking me if that would be a problem. But as I sat reflecting on the contrast between these two schools, it occurred to me that in New York, we tended to think more in terms of ethnicity than race. Maybe that is why the Lakewood principal's question seemed so odd.

In New York City, our identities were more closely tied to countries of origin. Yes, the white kids were white, but they generally characterized themselves in terms of culture as well. They weren't just white; they were Italian, Irish, Jewish, or the newly arrived Czechs, Lithuanians, and other Eastern Europeans. Many still spoke the languages of their countries of origin, although most were born in New York. In fact, none of the white kids I knew identified solely as white. This was also true with many of the blacks, Latinos, and Asians. My high school in New York had a mix of East Indians, West Indians, Haitians, Puerto Ricans, Black Americans, Dominicans, Cubans, Chinese, Pakistanis, and a host of others. Where I came from, ethnic difference was the norm. Getting along was a given. No one would even think to ask students if they thought they could get along because of an ethnic difference. We were immersed in ethnic difference. Everyone saw themselves as belonging to an ethnic group and the term "ethnic" wasn't used as a euphemism for "not white," at least not in my New York community in the mid-70s.

All but two were white? What did that mean? What was this experience going to be like? I was about to find out. In the days that followed, we began our new routine. My sister and I would take a bus provided by the school district. We'd have to wait for the bus at a designated corner on Pacific Coast Highway (PCH) – a stop that was further from my grandparents' home than was the local school. The bus would pick us up and deliver us to school each morning. At the end of the school day, the same bus would return us to the corner on PCH.

That first morning we got up early—a lot earlier than usual— so that we could catch the bus. This was one of those mornings with fog so thick you could barely see your hand in front of your face. We found the designated corner, stood waiting in the thick fog. It was a little eerie and a lot scary. With hardly another soul visible, my 14-year-old sister and I stood on a corner on Pacific Coast Highway as the sun began to rise and waited for the school bus.

Through the fog, the vision of a very large public bus right out of the 1950s slowly came into focus. Turns out it wasn't a school bus at all, at least not the typical yellow bus that usually takes children to school. No, this looked more like the bus Ralph Cramden drove in the 1950s sitcom "The Honeymooners." The words "school bus" weren't to be found anywhere on its dingy blue/gray exterior. Except for the driver, a tiny African American woman who looked to be about 18, the bus was empty. She pulled up, opened its squeaky door and said, "Come on in." I didn't know it then, but I'd just met my first California friend.

This just didn't add up. Why would the school district arrange to have a full-sized public bus transport two kids round trip from Long Beach to Lakewood five days a week during one of the worst oil crises in the history of this country? It was autumn of 1973. Fuel prices were through the roof. The Organization of Arab Petroleum Exporting Countries—typically called OPEC— had proclaimed an oil embargo against the United States. Cars were lined up around the block to get gas. Half the gas stations were running out.

In the weeks that followed, I began to put the pieces together. The local school in my grandparents' neighborhood wasn't overcrowded at all. My sister and I were being shuffled across town to solve a problem that wasn't even on our radar. We had walked right into a national controversy. In the mid-1970s, there was a heated national debate over the use of mandatory busing as a tool to increase racial balance in the nation's schools. Busing was enacted as a component of many schools' desegregation programs in response to federal court decisions establishing that racial segregation of public schools violated the Equal Protection Clause of the Fourteenth Amendment. In Green v. County School Board (1968), and Swann v. Charlotte-Mecklenburg Board of Education (1971), the Supreme Court established that federal courts could require schools to implement busing programs as a means of achieving racial integration.

The Long Beach Unified School district had a big problem. Racial segregation in the district was the norm. It was as bad as it had been in the Deep South under the old apartheid system—just as bad as it had been during the Jim Crow era. But wasn't this 1973? My racial consciousness was beginning to form.

I attended Lakewood High School from September 1973 to June of 1974. During that single school year, I learned more about the many variations of racism than all the previous 16 years of my life combined. To begin with, the desegregation program only bused black kids who were new to the community. But the busing was one-way. Believe me, there wasn't a bus that carried white students to black high schools. Busing was only mandatory for the black students who had recently moved into the community.

A few months after school started, the impact of the OPEC oil embargo kicked in full force. To save energy, Congress enacted the Emergency Daylight Saving Time Energy Conservation Act of 1973 which meant daylight savings time would be implemented year-round. Under different circumstances I probably wouldn't have paid attention to this new law. But that year, my sister and I were already leaving the house at 6:15 am. With the year-round time change, we were in effect leaving at

5:15 am. We were two girls walking half a mile every morning, a full hour and a half before sunrise. We got our share of unwanted offers for a free ride, always from creepy men. Cars that slowed as they passed were always cause for increased anxiety.

There was one bus that took us to school in the morning and one that brought us back to Long Beach at the end of the school day. If you missed either of those buses, you were out of luck. Of course, there were no cell phones back then. Getting stuck meant you had no way of getting in touch with anyone at home. This made it difficult for bused students to fully participate in school life. If I had an interest in an extracurricular activity— debate club, cheerleading, yearbook, football, the school newspaper, or drama club— too bad for me because those groups met either before or after school hours. Several of the core classes also required that the students spend at least some time working on projects together before or after school hours.

Because I was determined to not allow this transportation thing to beat me, I came up with some creative solutions of my own. When I needed to attend a rehearsal or meeting that just couldn't be missed, I'd often take public transportation home instead of using the school bus. But this required money, which I often didn't have. So, I got to know a couple of the city bus drivers. When I asked, they'd let me ride for free.

I discovered two major differences between taking a public bus in New York and taking one in Lakewood. The mere act of standing at a bus stop in New York never attracted attention because there were so many people standing with you, not so in Lakewood. Seems no one was ever waiting for a public bus in Lakewood. Sitting at a bus stop made you very noticeable. Often, while I sat waiting, men driving by (it was always men) would stop to ask if I'd like a ride. That never happened in New York. The second major difference between riding public transportation in New York and riding public in Lakewood was that the buses in New York always showed up, not so in Lakewood.

There wasn't a single direct route between my grandparents' house and Lakewood, so if I stayed after school and took the public bus instead of the school bus, I'd have to take two buses using a transfer. On one such trip, I was waiting for the second bus, in the middle of nowhere, when a man in a car stopped to offer me a ride. I turned him down. Two hours later the same man drove up. He stopped to offer a ride again. This time I accepted. Sadly, this occasionally became a way to get to and from school if the school bus wasn't available. I was very lucky that nothing terrible happened to me. But also, during that year, there were students, teachers, and that wonderful school bus driver named Wanda who made my experience tolerable most of the time. Turned out Wanda wasn't 18—she was a 28-year-old mother of five. Unfortunately, there were just as many who made it almost more than a 16-year-old should have to bear.

It doesn't take much imagination to conclude that I experienced my share of racial incidents and, yes, I did. But a couple were noteworthy and particularly hurtful to a teenager who didn't have a clue about the deeply entrenched racial divide that exists in this country. Here's one.

I was in an advanced social studies class that contained some of the top students in the school. I loved this class because the teacher encouraged open debate on current events and social commentary. Unlike the other classes, perhaps because of the open dialogues, I had developed friendships in this class. One day, I happened to spot one of those friends handing out a small envelope to the other students. Our eyes met. She saw that I saw that she was doing something that she didn't want me to see. To her credit, she was enough of a friend to tell me what was going on. It seems she was throwing a birthday party and was handing out the party invitations. She expressed deep regret that I would not be invited because her parents would not allow me in their home. This was not the only time this happened. As I write this, I still feel a little of the sting I felt on that day.

Another incident put things in a whole different perspective for me. This experience helped me to see that what I was observing at Lakewood was preparing me for life in these United States.

We were working on a group project in this same advanced social studies class. We had broken up into groups of four and were given a writing assignment. One of the requirements was that the paper we wrote had to have contemporary social relevance. Research for the paper was to be conducted as a team. My group consisted of two boys and two girls. Living during this national controversy and experiencing the sting of it firsthand, I suggested that we do something on the topic of racial integration. So, the four of us came up with a plan. Cal State Long Beach wasn't far from Lakewood High School. The two girls would pretend to be recent Cal State Long Beach grads apartment hunting. The boys had cars, so their job was to provide transportation, leads to apartment vacancies in Lakewood, help in tabulating the results, and input in the overall writing of the paper.

Lori (not her real name) and I would be the apartment hunting college girls. Lori and I were the same height, size and age. The biggest difference was race. The plan was that we'd both fill out and submit applications at the same apartment complexes. I'd apply first and she'd show up a few hours or, at most, a day later. We decided that the girls were more suited to play the role of college grads because, although the four of us were 16, the boys didn't look as mature as the girls. We didn't think they could pass for 22, the approximate age we figured we'd be if we'd just graduated. The other advantage was that I was black, and Lori was white. Both boys were white—an obvious disadvantage for this kind of experiment.

As 16-year-olds, both Lori and I were excited and nervous about whether we could pull this off. Our initial concern was that the apartment managers wouldn't believe we were college grads. Both of us decided to wear make-up, high heels, and borrowed clothes from an older sister in Lori's case and my Mom in mine.

In the first attempt, the four of us drove to our target. My three classmates stayed in the car a half a block away as I nervously approached the apartment building where a sign clearly advertised a vacancy. I rang the doorbell of the unit marked, "Manager." An older white woman opened the door. Through the screen I sensed a kind disposition. I believe she addressed me as "dear." Heaving a sigh of relief when she didn't seem to question my age, I didn't mind when the nice lady explained that she'd love to take my application, but unfortunately, the apartment had just been rented. She wished me luck as I went on my way feeling a bit victorious.

When I got back to the car, I told my classmates the details. We were all thrilled—we'd pulled it off! The way we planned it, I'd go to about four places and then we'd circle back so that Lori could go to the same places. Our initial fear turned out to be a non-issue. I now had more confidence about looking older—heck, I wondered if I could get into a nightclub. But for now, I'd keep my mind on getting to the next place. After each visit we documented things like the race, gender and approximate age of the apartment manager, the nature of the exchange (were they pleasant or rude, for example), and the look and feel of the place. The four of us felt we had the makings of a good project even though all the places I went to had just been rented. We were simply interested in completing the process and documenting the experience. We were sure we'd get a passing grade.

I was pleasantly surprised that, without exception, all the apartment managers were polite. They all encouraged me to keep looking, congratulated me on finishing college, and wished me luck in my future. My other team members were less surprised. They never expected our experiment to turn out to be a major sting operation. They were pretty sure Lori and I would get the same treatment, but they agreed that it was a good idea for a project, nevertheless.

After I'd gone to four rentals, we circled back so that Lori could follow the same sequence. At the first apartment complex, Lori was greeted by the same apartment manager who called me "dear." The same nice lady opened the door but—unlike my exchange which was held through a closed screen door—Lori was invited inside. The same woman who told me that the vacancy was filled gave Lori a tour of a vacant apartment.

She handed Lori an application and asked her to have a seat at the kitchen table to complete the application. This same woman promised Lori she'd get back to her within a week. Lori left the unit buoyed.

When she got back to the car, the boys and I were ready to document the exchange. When Lori told us what happened, the three of us were over the moon excited. What seemed like a project that would get us a passing grade was quickly looking like a guaranteed "A." We knew we'd hit a home run. All of us, myself included, were academically competitive. We wanted to get an "A," and this outcome almost assured us of that.

In the end, all four of the places that told me they had just rented the apartment—all four—took Lori's application. The first time this happened, I was just as excited as the rest of my team. But with each new revelation, I felt as if I were being kicked in the stomach. My teammates were oblivious to the depth of my disappointment, disgust, and despair. We were all taking a glimpse into our not-too-distant futures. Mine looked a lot bleaker than theirs through no fault of any one of us.

My team got an "A" on the project. Aside from giving us an "A," the teacher didn't discuss what we'd experienced. The teacher and my fellow students acted like this was just a school project. I seemed to be the only one who was keenly aware that we were all getting a glimpse into the reality of how inequality plays out. Heck, I was living it by being bused that entire year, walking in the dark constantly fearing we'd encounter unwanted attention from creepy men, being excluded from birthday parties, seeing first-hand how the nice landlords had no problem lying to me, all of this to remedy a national problem with a one-sided solution while my white counterparts' lives didn't miss a beat.

But here's the thing. None of us had a hand in creating the climate that fostered the kind of outcome our school project yielded, yet we were all beneficiaries of it. I received an unearned disadvantage—Lori received an unearned advantage – this was my introduction into seeing first-hand what we now call white privilege. I wish it had been my last.

Tic-Toc
by Alexander Gonzalez

April 20th, 2019: I am reading the story "An Amazing Woman" in my ESL 3B class. It made me remember the day of June 26, 2016.

On that day, I had been studying for two months at Los Angeles City College, but I couldn't pay my rent where I lived with my 13-year-old daughter because the college would not pay me until the 30th of July. I was supposed to pay the rent on June 10th. I did not have another job at this moment. I was working as a volunteer at the middle school where my daughter studied, but I did not have a salary.

Where I lived with my daughter, two men lived there as well. These men rented the room to me. They rented us one room for me and my daughter, and the restroom was shared. When I arrived at the house with my daughter, the restroom was closed, but my daughter needed to go the restroom. This was more important to me. However, the two men would not give my daughter permission to enter.

"Why?" I asked.

Them: "You did not pay the rent."

"My daughter needs to use the restroom," I answered.

Them: "We do not care."

7:35 pm: I go with my daughter to the room, and I call the police. Fifteen minutes later, the police arrived at the house. I spoke with the police about the situation. The police spoke to the two men and they left.

My daughter said to me, "Dad, I'm scared."

When the police left, the two men began to hit each other because they wanted to accuse me of having struck them.

I question, "Why? OH MY GOD!"

Them: "Because you did not pay us the rent."

10:35pm: Immediately, I call the police and tell the 911 operator what they were doing and what they wanted to do. I locked myself in the room with my daughter to wait for the police.

I heard the police siren and opened the door of the room. All the house lights were off. My daughter and I, at this moment, we were afraid. I was nervous. We saw one policeman enter the house with a lantern in his hand and a gun in the other. He walked towards our room and when he arrived to the door, we saw the gun was ready to shoot.

My daughter hugged me crying. The policeman, at that moment, lowered the gun and put it in its case.

I see the policeman and say, "We're leaving."

Police: "Ok, where are you going?"

I said, "With my friend Mario Pacheco. He has an office on the corner of Sunset and McCadden Place."

11:45 pm: We walk to the exit, and we see the two men speaking with more police. The police say to me, "Ok, go with your friend and come back tomorrow for your things." I needed more support from the police.

"OH MY GOD!" I thought. We walked down the street with lots of fear. I checked my watch and at that moment it was 12:30am. We thought everything was okay.

When we arrived at my friend's office, he called the one responsible for the office so they would open the door.

We decided not to return for our things at the house because it was better that way. We did not want more problems.

We could have been arrested. We have never been in jail for any reason, and at that moment, my daughter needed me more than the things that those men stole from us.

After living in a shelter and other places, my daughter is now 16 years old, and I'm 60 years old. We live in a small room where I pay per month. My daughter will finish high school next year, and maybe I will have a better job.

In conclusion, our life has changed because today I have a better job at Los Angeles City College.

"Night Lights"
(m. spray paint and white-ink pen on paper)
by Soosung An

On the Way—Driving
by Gilaine Fiezmont

I am waiting
for the mist
to cloud over
these skies.

I am waiting
for its mysteries
to inspire joy

> the man holding
> his toddler's hand
> at seven-thirty
> on Mission Street,
> clear blue light
> a brilliant invasion
> of Lincoln Park,
> the white walls
> cut the sky
> remind me of Babylon
> with Judy recounting
> > They had to cut
> > the abscess in his throat
> > and he screamed
> > But tell me
> > Why won't he learn English?
> and it's not
> that screams sound better
> in Spanish, no
> that isn't it at all.

I am waiting
for the moment

when I drop
this coat of sadness.

The memories mix
with the rain
glittering on the
green dewed morning
breaths I catch
the vision a second
                        time driving past
            the athlete shadowboxing
            his imaginary foe
            jogging on the corner
            of Fifth Street and
            Figueroa until
            the light turns green
            in this
                        the city of our Lady
Queen of the Angels
where David remembers
            How long I looked for them,
            the angels of San Gabriel
Sang Sanskrit verse
or was it Arabic?
He danced into the dusk
lured them to him at last and
in the end it's not
what people say down
south, keeping God to
themselves, no
it's not that at all.

Night falls with
Rubies and Diamonds

sprinkled across my eyes
they dance, a glimmering
drawn-out snake
of stars lit up
one moment, faint the next.

I break, avoid
familiar hazards
but not, no longer
quite so quickly
my mind droning
my heart pumping in rhythm
with the radio drowning out
this quiet, clearly drawn out

                              sigh

I'll live with from now on.
A touch, a finger across
my cheek like a tear
like the burst
of soft warmth
when a human voice
caresses your ear.

I have struggled
with you, the taste
of your love
faded
        like the lights in
        my rear-view mirror
blinding me briefly until
the cars have passed and
darkness soothes me further down the road.

My Twenties Love Summed Up as a Child
by Kevin Matson

I didn't have a sandcastle bucket,
so we use drink cups
from my mom's cabinet.
We build for four hours
poking the mounds with small sticks,
the rollercoaster and Santa Monica Pier behind us
as our backdrop.
The sand beneath us –
the yard castle dwellers play in.
The castle dwellers are the shells
who now inhabit more than the ocean's beach,
they walk the corridors
of the sandcastle's long hallways we placed them in.
We give them names.
Molly
and Cashmere.
Together we play
deep into the tide.
We dig out a mote to stop the waves.
It is immense and carved from sun burnt skin.
Before the waves take to the mote,
you step on the house we built
together.
The sand no longer seems
like the front yard
the castle dwellers play in.
I tell you you're a booger picker dummy.
I feel the sand in my swimsuit.
It's itchy and uncomfortable.
I want to go home.

Return of the Angels
by Erick Marcia

The City of Angels in a state of confusion,
As it dies by the hands of our own pollution.
The epidemic grows worse, walks with pride,
Makes sure to step on those who lay on the side
Of the street, don't got nothing to eat.
Ignore them! Nothing but a nuisance,
Walk by! Don't even spare a few cents.
Want to bring back the beauty of the show,
So, dump them all at Skid Row.

Show them the lights, so they'll enjoy their stay,
Bring back the beauty of Broadway.
Open a Starbucks, or maybe two,
Throw in some Air Jordans 'cause they love that shoe.
Next step: Get rid of Pepe's and Leon's!
Fill the streets with all of its peons,
Got their heads in the iCloud,
City gets covered in a dark shroud.

Night flows, with a wonderful dream,
Smiling from the destruction in Chavez Ravine.
Another thought, of something ecstatic,
Why not haunt those who saw Kareem and Magic?
A new stadium in Inglewood, double their rents,
Maybe they end up living in tents.

What is this? Someone tryin' to do good?
The solution is to close the schools in the hood.
Want more money, want to go on field trips?
Let's see how they enjoy them pink slips.
They're learning? Beginning to bloom?

Shove them all in the same classroom!
Oh, now they want to barter?
Too late, the money has gone to charter.
The city lays there, filled with delight,
Without a worry in the slight.

Night goes on, a child lays at rest.
Her mother gets up, hoping for the best.
She's an alien, can't get a good job,
Her child's future rests on a bacon wrapped hot dog.
A father rises, filled with so much pain,
Continues with construction, his children with so much to
Gain. They escape their country, endure the mayhem,
Hoping their children can have a future in STEM.

City of Angels suddenly wakes filled with dread,
Sees a massive ocean filled with red.
They've come together, know their rights?
Didn't think they could put up a fight.
They march down the streets, one fit for a King,
City wonders who could've come up with such a dreadful
Thing? Its head becomes light, it hears an awful clatter,
A furious roar chanting "Black Lives Matter."
It's shocked, thought it was but a rustle,
When it sees those united by the Hussle.
It's lost, doesn't know what to do,
Loses all hope when it hears "Me Too."

This City filled with a plague,
Is showing it isn't on its last leg.
Communities unite, know the truth,
Everything must be done to save the youth.
Fight's been long, the outcome uncertain,
But this great city is once again filling with Angels.

The Comfort Tamales
by Veronica Chavira

Steam kissed my sneaky hand
As my Mama pinched my curious cheek.
"No Tocas, mijia," she said sternly.

Mi Familia in December
Annual assembly line tradition:
Corn husks
Masa
Spreading
Mole
Meat
Wrapping

Tias, Tios, Madre y Padre
Spreading on masa smoothly on each leaf
Not too little, not too much
A serious job for adults only

Primas, Hermano y Yo
Adding the meat or queso to the center
I sat distracted eating the black olives out of the can
One by one on each finger
One by one in my mouth
One happily dived into a tamale

"Ay, Dios Mio! Twelve dozen in one day," I said.
My Tia laughed, "That's nothing."

Three ollas birthed warm gifts:
Steam rising
Teasing our noses

Unwrapping
Eating
Gorging
Embracing a pansa

Smell of masa hugs our clothes
Tamales exploded out of the refrigerator
We stored the favorites in the freezer
A delicious memory con Mi Familia

"Immediate Disposal"
(m. black-ink on watercolor paper)
by Maria L. Caballero

Life Stories from the Inside/Out
Introduction by Marlene McCurtis

For nine weeks this spring, I and three other TheatreWorkers Project teaching artists make our way up Highway 14, climbing two thousand feet above sea level to the California State Prison, Los Angeles County (LAC) in Lancaster. The city of Lancaster is 75 miles from Downtown Los Angeles. It is the high desert out there on the far northern reaches of Los Angeles County in the Mojave. The land is flat and dry, a valley surrounded by the San Gabriel and Tehachapi mountain ranges. Some days there is a chill and a wind blowing across the desert floor, but other days the air is still, the sun bright against a cloudless sky as we unload our van and bring our notebooks, pens, props, water bottles and open hearts inside the prison to teach theatre, writing and movement to a group of inmates housed in the Progressive Programming Facility or the "A yard." In order to live on this yard, the inmates must disavow their gang affiliations. They can't adhere to the self-imposed prison rule to racially segregate, and they must stay drug and alcohol free. There are numerous educational, therapeutic and vocational opportunities on "A yard." It is a place for healing and transformation.

Each Wednesday, we gather for four hours in the prison chapel on "A yard" with twenty-three inmates all dressed in identical blue shirts and elastic-waisted denim pants. In this chapel, a refuge from prison life, we are all "artists" as TheatreWorkers Project's founder and director, Susie Tanner, always reminds us and the participants. Over the course of nine weeks, with gentle guidance from the teaching artists, the men courageously explore and examine their lives through writing, theater exercises and physical theater expression. They then use their writing as a framework to create a spoken word theater and movement performance piece which they present to invited guests, prison staff and their fellow inmates at a culmination event.

Many of the inmates we work with have life sentences; several have Life Without Parole. Most committed their crimes in their late teens or early twenties and have grown up in prison. They have worked hard at examining their lives, their mistakes and what led them to commit their crimes. In this place, where each day they are reminded they are incarcerated without the freedoms most of us on the outside take for granted, they have found hope, joy, resilience, self-respect, patience, redemption, laughter, artistic expression and deep, deep gratitude. We are reminded of their appreciation after each weekly workshop when every single man either fist bumps or shakes each teaching artist's hand to say good-bye and then thanks us for making the time to share our artistic skills with them. One of TheatreWorkers Project's goals is to create an ensemble where the participants can build trust and take creative risks. The men we work with have done that and more. They inspire each other and us. Their joy has become our joy. Their patience and perseverance have deepened our own patience and commitment to strive despite obstacles.

There are many strong writers in the group and the writing included here is just a small sampling of their work. Several of the pieces are inspired by writing exercises given to the men during the nine-week workshop. A few like "Babylon is Falling" by Lester Polk and "Emergence" by Louie Brash are featured in the final performance piece. "Standing Count" by James Heard is a direct result of a rather brash inmate count that interrupted one of our workshops. During this count, each man is required to stand up when his last name is called by a prison Correctional Officer and to say the last two numbers of his inmate identification number. Keeping count of inmates is an important part of prison security, but it is also a reminder to each man that he is a number, less than human. It is particularly jarring during a workshop when for a few hours the inmates and even we forget the barbed wire and metal gates just outside the chapel doors. After the count, Heard wrote this poem and shared it with the group. Its emotional immediacy and truth moved us all.

For now, my trek up the 14 is over. This fall, I plan to continue working with TheatreWorkers Project's *Life Stories from the Inside/Out,* and the brave men on "A yard." I hope you find their work as beautiful and authentic as we do. *Life Stories from the Inside/Out* is funded by the California Arts Council Arts in Corrections initiative with support from the California Department of Corrections and Rehabilitation (CDCR).

Judgment Day
by Justin S. Hong

I sit with my co-defendant, David, in the small holding tank just outside courtroom 121 in the Los Angeles Criminal Courts Building. These enclosures are usually filled with loud chatter and cluttered with blue, yellow, and green smocks. However, today we have the tank to ourselves, and it is unnervingly quiet. We have already changed out of our county blues and into our "trial clothes," a routine we have been following for the past few weeks. David is dressed in his Army uniform, dark green with colorful patches commemorating his accomplishments. I sport a burgundy dress shirt, grey slacks and a grey jacket, looking like a boy who crawled into his father's suit.

The walls are covered with gang insignia that has been etched and scratched into the chipping paint. Plastic bags, apple cores, and smashed peanut butter packets litter the floor beside the toilet and in the corners. David is hunched over, zealously flipping through his Bible to find a verse to encourage himself. I close my eyes to try to find a moment of peace in the midst of my chaotic thoughts. After a year in the county jail and a month-long trial, the verdict is in. Our jury only took 30 minutes to reach a decision.

"I don't think that's a good sign," David utters bleakly.

I quickly rebut his rational thinking with a hopeful exuberance. "No, it's a good sign David! It means our innocence is obvious. There's nothing to worry about."

Still, my confidence is clouded by the internal storm that is raging within me. "It's finally over David. We're going home," I say more for me than for him. I

69

open my eyes as I hear the jiggling of keys find their way into the keyhole. The lock turns with a loud *clack*, followed by the loud mechanical hum of the electric barrier opening our way to an uncertain fate. The bailiff signals us to step out of the holding tank and into the courtroom.

As I find my way to the seat beside my lawyer, my family gives me a weary smile. They have been through hell in the nightmare I created yet continue to bear the excruciating heat. Beside my mother and sister, David's family and friends look on with hopeful smiles. There are others in the gallery as well. Separated by a couple of rows, a mother, a brother, and other family members sit in stoic silence as they stare down their son's murderers.

My lawyer, Mr. Fountain, grey-haired with dark circles under his eyes, scribbles on his notepad. He gives me a quick glance. "Let's hope for the best," he says as he returns to his notes. I twiddle my thumbs as the judge and jury walk back into the courtroom.

"Will the defendants please rise?" the bailiff says.

Feeling as if I am in an episode of *Law and Order*, I stand, flexing my knees to stabilize my footing. I look towards David and give him a reassuring nod. *Everything is going to be okay.* But my stomach is in knots. I close my eyes and whisper the words I wish to hear, "*Not guilty, not guilty.*"

The judge asks the jury if they have reached a verdict. "Yes, your Honor, we have." The foreman hands my judgment to the bailiff, which he carries like a secret to the judge. I hear the magistrate read off my charges. "*Not guilty, not guilty,*" I whisper.

"On the count of first-degree murder, the members of the jury find the defendants...GUILTY." My body goes numb. My ears pop and my hearing is dull as if *I* am under water. David collapses into his chair, his face blank with fear and shock. The world collapses around me.

"I'm innocent!" I scream, hoping someone will believe me. My plea is futile as the judge demands I take a seat. As I sit down, I look to the gallery and see my mother's face, lifeless and in disbelief. My sister is crying, her 15-year-old mind grasping the reality that her brother will not be coming home. I can hear Mr. Fountain saying something about an appeal, but a single thought repeats in my head like a broken record: *My life is over. My life is over. My life is over.* The bailiff escorts David and me back into the holding tank.

"I knew something was wrong. They came with the verdict too fast," David says, his voice quick and short of breath. I stare at David as he paces back and forth. My brain cannot process what just happened. *My life is over. My life is over. My life is over.*

After we change into our county blues, a deputy unlocks the door. "Hong! Kim! Let's go!" David and I follow the deputy towards the elevator. We are taken down to the garage where a Los Angeles County Jail bus awaits us. Handcuffed and chained, we enter the cold vehicle. As we pull out of the dark garage, the sun's light offers me a glimmer of hope. I look towards David sitting beside me, his face downcast as he clutches his Bible. As I pass through the familiar streets of Los Angeles back towards the county jail, the clouds suddenly cover the sun, blanketing the world with darkness. *My life is over. My life is over. My life is over.*

Babylon Has Fallen
by Lester Polk

Babylon has fallen
Babylon has fallen

A world ends in a single night
Childhood extinguished
A lifelong trauma begins

     A Mark
          A Blemish
               A Stigma
Lifelong Pain!
Dynamic Intrusion
Psychotic Confusion
Safety Illusion

Not here, not there
          Despair
               Despair
Square Peg
          Round Hole

               Dark Stain on Soul
Abyss
Sinking
Darkness surrounds
Suffocating Blackness
Babylon has Fallen

          Who will lift him up?

          Who will lift him up?

Only If the Door Had Been Opened
by Deville Simmons

Father, your idea of being a dad was keeping a roof over my head and food in my stomach. But, there is more to it than that. Time is everything. Spending time with a son is very important.

Who do you think taught me to tie my shoes?
It wasn't you.

Who do you think taught me to how to play ball?
It wasn't you.

Who do you think taught me about sex and how to treat a woman? It wasn't you.

Who do you think taught me how to protect myself?
It wasn't you.

The funny thing is, you were there in the next room over with your door always closed, doing you. So, the streets taught me what you didn't.

I wonder how things would have turned out, if only you had opened your bedroom door.

STANDING COUNT!
by James Heard

Standing count! Last two and sit down.

What, no "excuse me"?

Lights on!

Did you know that "the wound is where the light enters"?

Standing count! Murderer, criminal, 1015!

Yes, I account for my actions....

Radio that nonsense. I said Standing Count!

I stand as a human being, accountable to the communities I serve.

Prone out!

Prone out? I only stand.

Not kneel. Not crawl or hide.

My existence stamped-out?

Never! My legacy...

I exist!

I rise up!

No Dream
by Jerimichael Cooley

Back flat on cold steel
Clangs sounding
Alarms peal
Weight of world presses down
Shackles of oppression holding ground.

All seems lost
No reason to dream
Light comes flooding in strong
Hand reaches down
Grabs hold, lifts-up.

Rising high, chains shatter
Smile is now taking over
Rising, leaping, nothing but joy
Family, friends, girls, boy
Light subdues, lopsided grin
It's my wife
And this is no dream.

I Am First
by Allen Burnett[1]

2217 West 9th Street, Santa Ana: that is our Grandma's house. I am first. She makes me, my little sister, and my little cousins memorize her address and phone number *just in case we get lost.* We love summers at Grandma's house; we do not go to school. We explore barefoot in our Grandma's backyard—we climb trees, run from her chickens, and poke sticks at her bees. We have rock fights, fig fights, mud fights—grass in our hair and stains on our knees and when we get too loud, our Grandma makes us hull peas. Our Grandma has a garden—she has hundreds of peas.

At night, we are dirty, and Grandma makes us shower and take baths. We do not sit at Grandma's table until our hands and faces are clean, and we do not eat until Papa comes home. Grandma cooks meatloaf and potatoes with cornbread and—peas. We always have peas.

Our Grandma's couch becomes a bed at night—it fits all seven of us right under the coo-coo clock. Those gears, they wind, whine, grind, tick, and click. We sleep cozy throughout the night, but when the rooster crows, I wake up just before six. I am first. I see my Grandma. She wears a blue housecoat and blue slippers. She moves slowly about her kitchen making little noise. She fries bacon and eggs; they pop and sizzle on her stove. She has her back to us. She does not see me, but she

---

[1] *On September 13, 2019, Governor Newsom granted executive clemency to Allen Burnett, commuting his Life Without Parole sentence. Burnett has been incarcerated for 27 years.*

knows I am awake. She makes one plate with buttered toast and grape jelly, brown eggs and bacon and sets it on the table for me because I am first. I follow the smell to the seat. Grandma sits across from me, and she watches me eat. Her food is good—it tastes like love. I love being first. I am always first. I am her first.

Granny's Cooking
by Donnell Campbell

Granny's cooking was always the best,
miles above all the rest.

Black eyed peas, mac & cheese, turtle soup
and collard greens.

Smoked hams, dirty rice, pinto beans and
candied yams.

The home smelled of exotic foods from
faraway places, putting smiles on many faces.

The chocolate cake stood five layers high,
a mountain of sweetness reaching for the sky.

The lemon meringue, apple, sweet potato
and peach pies shine bright like Granny's eyes.

Banana pudding and peach cobbler didn't last long,
like the ending of a beautiful song.

Granny's cooking made magical moments in time. She's
in heaven now, but these memories are forever mine.

Recipe for "Sweet Love"
by Jermaine Pina

Take 2 people (peeled and washed of all expectations)
Marinade in 2 cups of Willingness
and 1 cup of complete Honesty
Mix in a bowl 2 tablespoons of Spicy Personality
2 tablespoons of Consideration with a ½ cup of Audacity
Stir in 10 fluid ounces of Quality Time…
let it sit for 2-3 hours
Pre-heat tests and trials until golden brown and firm
(Be sure to turn People up and down and all around to
guarantee even cooking)
Allow to rest on the rack after frying
While still hot—sprinkle with Selflessness, Genuineness
and Sugary Kisses
Serve at room temperature
(Note: Sweet Love's Flavors intensify and deepen over
time, so take time---and enjoy.)

Emergence
by Louie Brash

I learned to accept who I was
revelation after revelation
self-serving attitude
stepping
into a furnace of fear, pain and addiction.
Feeling
not running.

Stillness like a quiet sky against a dark night
Embracing like a mother's love
Being open like the light from the sun
Hoping for something better
Loving in a way I never knew.
I am reborn
as someone who is whole.
I am new.
I am enough.

"Safe within Empyrean Apparatuses"
(m. graphite on paper)
by Adrian Garcia

Cowboy Says
by Gregory Raygoza

When the Earth pivots slowly before one's eyes back toward the sun and all the nocturnal creatures recede from the day, the veil of darkness that guards sinners and criminals from the eyes of decent people is lifted. When morning comes and lays its heat on the ground for yet another day, there is a certain truth that is laid bare. This is the harsh light of day. Cowboy watched this slow transition every day from behind the morning paper, leaning against the wall of the corner donut shop, sometimes a pen in hand finishing a crossword puzzle. She'd watch the neon signs fade into the sunlight as good, honest people stretched and yawned, squinting their eyes at the world. And as each day came, so came with it the violent jostling of garbage trucks and buses, their shrill brakes that cut the silence in half, their exhaust pipes leaving the air thick with soot. The streets illuminated, trash scuttling along the floor in the wind, and there among it all, unmoved, was Cowboy.

Just shy of six feet, Cowboy was built like a stallion, proudly displaying her haunches in a pair of stretch pants, a small, soft stomach peeking out from under a frilly off-the-shoulder blouse. Atop her mulleted hair rested a cowboy hat, whose shadow softened a rather handsome face. She could have given the Marlboro man a run for his money.

Cowboy was indefinitely housed in the Wonderland Motel on the corner of Garvey and Rosemead. The Wonderland was across the street from Bill's Palace, a local bar frequented by bums, hookers, and down-and-out day laborers. Logistically, Garvey was a great street for prostitutes. It was the main thoroughfare that ran through the entire length of town, a decent gateway to Los Angeles about fifteen miles west. Its cross street, Rosemead, was an exit for two major freeways. A lonely traveler could easily find company in the sea of burnt out beauties and finish his route without too much suspicion. Cowboy had seen many girls come and go over the years, never indulging in the sorority of gossip and war stories. Her even temper came off as cold to some girls but that didn't bother her. Her conscience was clean. She minded her own business and expected others to do the same, but she did have a soft spot for Michael.

Cowboy and Michael weren't close, but they were friendly. He was kind to her, and she reciprocated his kindness, as neighbors do. As Michael made his way to school, Cowboy would be there to give him an encouraging word, and on his way back home he'd often pass by her to relay the day's lessons. She'd listen kindly and engage, although she was always on the clock and would not hesitate to leave him in mid-sentence if a car pulled over to the side of the road. When this first happened, Michael was infuriated and insulted. He ran to mother, to tell her how rude Cowboy had been, "She's gotta make a living," she said plainly.

On a particularly brutal day, when the sidewalk was baked a blinding white, Michael saw Cowboy standing in her usual spot, looking a little wilted, some old bruises on her white skin bursting into soft shades of yellow. She was sweating out her vices and smelled a bit stale. He tried his best not to stare at her but failed. He knew how humiliating it was for a beaten woman to walk the streets, eyes staring at her with a pity usually reserved for crippled animals.

Victor, Cowboy's husband and pimp, had no

doubt roughed her up again. Cowboy and Victor shared the same addictions, but Cowboy was the primary bread winner. Victor was on disability and his meager check could hardly carry them both (though his pride was greater than both of them). He was a short Mexican with a thick mustache and a glass eye. His voice was almost as raspy as Cowboy's, although much lower. One had to lean in close to make out what Victor was saying but few people felt safe doing so, and he'd learned long ago to remain mostly quiet. Whereas Cowboy's silence came with confidence, Victor's composure was full of a quiet anxiety and suspicion. Garvey Avenue was thick with men like him, men who had squandered the strength of their youth and mental tenacity on violence. Erratic and frequent periods of incarceration engineered their bodies for violence with a mean, undefined muscle. They patrolled the streets, taking what they believed was rightfully theirs, namely everything. But as time went on, their bodies grew weaker and their minds more weary. Their proud gaits gradually became slow limps. Their voices, burnt by smoke and drugs, became husky, unintelligible slurs. Their infirmity preceded their every step, and they were often dismissed by others on the streets as old fools.

Victor had once told Cowboy that his greatest fear was that his years of murder and violence would catch up with him in the afterlife. He cried at night, fearing he'd never be reunited with his dead mother, who suffered her entire life worrying for her son. He screamed himself awake some nights dreaming vivid, distorted, and fantastic memories of the destruction he had left behind. Cowboy would jolt up and shake him awake, freeing him from his nightmares. She'd cradle him and he'd cling to her sobbing. She'd hold him, and when he was safely back to sleep then she would fall asleep too.

It was a mystery to Michael why a woman of Cowboy's stature would allow a man as cowardly and pathetic as Victor to lay hands on her. She could destroy him. Victor had dragged her out of Bill's Palace to beat her in front of god and everyone. She had been working all night and morning and stopped in for a drink, but Victor wasn't keen on her drinking up their drug money. No one stopped him as he beat her on the hot pavement. It was nobody's business but their own. Cowboy braced herself until it was done, never fighting back once, even when he kicked her face (which she knew would cost them both later). She knew he needed it, to blow off some steam, to feel that he was still a man. She took on the burden of his weakness and anger and bore his fear across her body.

Seeing Cowboy there that afternoon, leaning against the wall with shaken dignity, Michael tried to pass by politely, unnoticed, as not to bother her, but she called out to him.

"Michael!" she shouted digging her hand deep into the hollows of his shoulder.

"Hey!" he shouted back smiling in pain, looking up at her silhouette eclipsing the sun.

"Whatchu got for me today, kid?"

"Nothing much."

"Humor me, little man. I haven't had a customer all day and this heat ain't doing much for me either."

He looked up to her and for the first time saw a sad, tired, old woman, a woman of few words and few friends. He saw a woman whose strength had its limits and whose silence called out for compassion. He didn't know what to say. What he wanted to say was *sorry* but he knew that she didn't want any cheap sympathy.

He offered her a brief history of the California missions, and western expansion, which he had learned about in school that day. She listened politely as he recalled to her that San Gabriel Valley was the end of the Santa Fe Trail, how it had a rich agricultural history, and was a blessing to weary travelers.

"Western expansion, huh?" she asked. "You know, I made that trip too."

"Really?!" he asked excitedly, imagining her ample body riding a white steed in front of a caravan of covered wagons.

"Yeah, lemme buy you a drink and I'll tell you all about it," she said propping herself off the wall.

They walked to a nearby liquor store. She bought a 40 oz. for herself and a Coca Cola for Michael. He felt the sugar and fizz kick in as they sat against the wall under a sliver of shade. Cowboy pulled out a cigarette, lit it, and took a much-deserved drag. She took a drink from a paper bag, sighed and spilled her guts.

Cowboy never minded Michael's age, always giving him the courtesy of speaking frankly, like a friend, which made him feel important. Today she was feeling especially chatty and she let her guard down in the heat and sadness, becoming much more candid than Michael had ever expected her to be. He was both worried and excited that she would speak with a liberty which she would later regret. *But maybe,* he thought, *she won't even remember.*

She grew up in a large Mormon family, she told Michael. Michael told her that two Mormon children had recently been transferred to his school and confided in her that he didn't know exactly what a Mormon was, but that the one's at his school were not too social with the other students.

"They're probably just nervous. Mormons are good people, charitable, patient..." she took a swig. "Most of them anyways, but there's always gonna be a few assholes wherever you go."

Her father was one of those assholes, she said, an alcoholic and a gambler, long abandoning the texts of the Golden Plates. She grew up in a small city near Vegas. Her father ran off to the city any chance he got for days at a time, coming home with empty pockets and pants full of sexual frustration. Cowboy, who was called Shannon then, was the second youngest of five daughters, a healthy lot for a pedophile like her dad. The family never discussed the abuse, and the home was paralyzed with fear and shame. As the years went on, the older girls were married off and her father became more feeble. The remaining family downsized to a two bedroom house in Pahrump. One night, Cowboy's younger sister woke up with a fever. She'd caught meningitis. After a week in the hospital, she was dead. Her father never touched Cowboy again. Her parents hardly talked. The apartment was gripped in a grim stagnation. Her sister's bed was never removed, and her mother, ever distant, became emotionally catatonic. Her father, already very ill himself, counted down his days till merciful death. Cowboy seized the moment, taking to the streets and finding adventure.

At seventeen she ran away from home to live with her first boyfriend, a belligerent heroin addict who'd suffered a major injury in minor league baseball. He put her on the streets. After two years together, he was busted for an armed robbery that went bad and got a ten-year sentence for attempted murder. By then both her parents had died and she'd no one to return to. She was alone and afraid, relatively green, and she needed guidance and protection on the streets. Her family life, however unconventional, was strangely sheltered, and she found the politics of street culture too complicated to make sense of. She had never been completely alone in her life and did not intend to stay that way. Within days of her boyfriend's arrest, she met Victor who was then a broad and able-bodied drifter, working his way around the Southwest. When he met Cowboy, she was still a tall, awkward child of a woman with icy blue eyes and sunburned skin. *She looks like a girl and makes love like a woman*, Victor bragged to his friends. Victor could see her potential. He was headed west to Los Angeles and asked if she wanted to tag along. Cowboy jumped at the chance to join him.

"I thought for a hot second that I might become a movie star!" she laughed. "Boy was I wrong!"

They spent a couple of exciting nights in LA but ended up settling in El Monte. The motel rooms there were cheaper. She and Victor had been there ever since.

By the time she was done reciting her story, Michael had finished his soda. His mouth felt sticky and dry with sugar, and the heat only made it worse.

Cowboy was quiet for a moment, chugging on her beer, making up for the time that she had been talking and not drinking. She still looked rough, but Michael could see that the beer was taking the edge off her.

He decided to take advantage of her drunkenness by asking a question that he wouldn't have courage to ask otherwise, "Cowboy," he asked, "how did Victor lose his eye?"

"I stabbed him in the face," she said as she got up and wobbled to the curb as a car had just pulled up. She hopped in the car and rode off with the stranger. Michael got up and made his way home.

The Milliners
by Breanna Barton-Shaw

On the top of a hill, after the trolley, through guest reception on the way to pick up an audio guide, across the blazing white tiles, one floor up the stairs of the West Pavilion, at the very back of the 18th century artists hall, nestled in the corner, is one of the finest paintings that no one ever sees. It's brown and ugly. Unappealing and dull. The subject is plain and if there are any details at all, they're sparse and bloated with revisions – so why do I feel so connected to it?

It's a simple painting of two women sitting at a desk making hats. The painting itself was named after them – The Milliners – and maybe it was interesting at first because I had to look up the word "milliner" and what it even meant. Milliner, noun, is a person who "designs, makes, trims, or sells women's hats." An entire term dedicated to an entire trade that no longer exists. Funny, I thought, and that was that.

I didn't know it yet, but my affair with the milliner had just begun. There was something about the sallow face of the forlorn woman between the two hat stands that charmed me.

She felt like the comfort of feeling sad, and I wanted to indulge myself, but it scared me. To me, she was dangerous; she was the last shot of gin, the final cigarette, the first step to my own plummet into what I could only explain as abysmal and unexplored by the living. So, I stepped away before I fell.

I was lost in the ecstasy of *Christ's Entry into Brussels* in the next building. James Ensor would be proud to have distracted me from my sad lady with modern excess and the humility of faith, but it wasn't for long. The bombastic commentary of Ensor's *Christ* should have thrilled me, but I was stuck on my lady. I had to get back.

She was right where I left her, and when I stepped into the artist's shoes, close enough to reach out and touch if I wanted my hand slapped, I felt awash in relief that she had stayed the same – maybe even grew more pitiful than how I'd remembered.

Her eyes were downcast and shadowed as she stared into the table and her thin, pinks lips were parted in a sigh that I could almost hear. It would be heavy but come mostly from her nose. It's not a wet, exhausted sigh, but one of resignation. It was a daily sigh at the peak of the hour when you realize no one will care what you make, only that you exist to embody a job no one wants. A job that doesn't even exist anymore.

She was a fossilized woman, stuck forever between a pair of hat stands and her own uselessness.

I listened to the audio guide and it broke my heart. She wasn't a milliner at the beginning. An x-ray of the oil paints told a story about the sad lady, how she used to have fancy collars and cuffs with a smile on her face and a need for a hat to be made for a party or a Sunday event. And then Degas changed his mind and sentenced her to forever sit behind that workbench and dream of what she used to be, if it had not been for the whim of an old man who thought luxury and status weren't as beautiful as destitution and emotional abatement.

Yes. That's the face of bitter circumstance. I'd seen it on my mother's face many times. Too many times. That look in the milliner's eyes is the only way I can remember my mother. Maybe that's why I couldn't get the painting out of my head.

Scouring the gift shop, I looked for a postcard to take with me. I kneeled at the wall of cards that featured precious paintings, even Degas' ballerinas, abdicating any pride in my search for the milliner. I found her at the top, watching the worship with downcast eyes.

I tacked the card onto the easel before I started to paint. I had to get it right, I had to capture that look and capture everything I could about my mother in that little milliner, or I would go crazy. I had to have just a piece of her returned.

Mom had been dead for quite a while now, and I could barely remember her face. That made it so much easier to lie to myself and say she and the milliner looked so alike. They both had thin lips, dark hair, pink cheeks and a harrowing look of resignation; they even had the same pallid green undertone. Mom always looked sickly and a little toxic, like the world was poisoning her blood, and she planned to poison it right back.

Canvas was best set by hand, someone told me, so I stretch it over a little wooden frame thinking of how lovely my own little sad lady will be. I didn't intend to copy. I just wanted that expression. Degas wanted Holbein's cheeks. I wanted my mother. Some mimicry is fine. With a rubber mallet, I banged in the pegs to finish the stretching, splashed some white primer, and spread thick the brown and red paint.

I called out to her with my brush and she ignored me, making me want her attention even more.

"Talk to me," I would say in the dark of the studio. "Why are you so sad?" The shaking voice of the girl I used to be made my throat give and my lips shake like a poorly made dam.

The last memory I had of my mother was a good one, or at least I'd twisted the reeds of a bad memory into a basket for my rose-colored nostalgia to gather dust. We were living in a tent but this time at a campground, so it wasn't as obvious the sheets of nylon and tarp were our only home. She had the milliner's face, or the milliner had her face. To me, Mom and the milliner were timeless: both existing and unreal at the same time. Mom was staring into the fire. Her eyes were downcast, her lips were between a sigh, her face just the bad side of ashen as she smoked a hand-rolled joint, and I asked her the very same:

"Why are you so sad?"

I didn't know she'd already been planning our separation. I had no idea she was staring into the fire that night trying to decide between pills or hanging. We were too poor to buy a gun and knives were too messy. Even in the firelight, Mom's eyes were shadowed like the sad milliner and, just like the milliner, she stayed silent.

She chose hanging. In a park restroom, no less.

I repainted. And painted. Over and over again, until, like Degas, it seemed to be 25 years I'd been working on this sad woman. I wouldn't stop until she was hallow-cheeked. I kept painting until her eyes were just the right amount of sad and cold, my brush set green to her cheeks and pink to her lips, and I sat back to look at her anew.

Still, she wasn't right.

Soon my brushstrokes worked a rhythm that wasn't my own. I wasn't taken by a madness, nor was I possessed by the spirit of Degas; I was overcome with a harrowing emptiness. Nothing I could do would bring Mom back, not even on canvas, not even in homage, as if I were forbidden to see her again even in my mind's eye. Her gaze evaded me, her shoulders were too sunken, her face was too green – she was a horror of my own making, and I loathed her. Hatred absolutely burned me.

Furious, I clawed through the fresh paint. I pushed and smeared her shallow eyes and her horrible cheeks. I forever closed her sighing mouth with a hard swipe of my palm because she never opened it to tell me *why*. I smacked the canvas to the ground, slapping the easel with it. With a clatter, it broke apart at the hinges, but I didn't care. Ripping off the postcard, I cried, "Tell me why you're so *fucking* sad!" and wondered how I would feel to get an answer – to *finally* know. She never left a note. She left nothing behind but this face in my delicate memory.

My hands were green with paint, and I went to wash them off. In the mirror, I saw my face. My mother's face. The milliner's face. I stared and stared until I couldn't tell if I was looking at myself or a sad woman who'd been dead for a long time. It could've been impossible to tell. Reaching up, I painted the mirror with my palm, touching it with spots of green and brown until there was nothing reflective left, until I'd snuffed out whatever light, whatever color, was left of me or Mom or the milliner, and I could forget it all in the smell of fresh oil paint and chalky sink water.

I could rip up my postcard and paint a thick white over my mess. I could forget the milliners and ignore the memories enlivened by smoke and park bathrooms. It's so easy in theory how much I don't have to think about it all.

But I can't.

I go back instead. I drive up the hill and take the trolley. I check in through guest reception and grab an audio guide for company. Crossing the blazing white tiles is a walk across hell this time of year, "How fitting," I think, as I walk the path of Orpheus. I take the stairs and ignore the Renaissance, the Impressionists. I'll visit Ensor's *Christ* later, and I beeline to the end of the 18th century hall.

There she sits, resolute and unmoving, snug in a corner and overlooked by the world like so many sad women are. I stand before her, taking my Degas spot, and ask again, "Why are you so sad?" I'm begging, pleading, for something.

Still, there's no answer. Nothing. Silence. And then an old woman shuffles to a stop beside me. She's made up of grey hair and grey lips that poked out from her complex skin, and she watched the milliner like an old friend who understood. This old woman had a lifetime to earn her understanding.

"That's just how she was painted," the old woman said with a sigh of resignation passing through her nose.

Was it as simple as that?

Self-Portrait

by Lorely Guzman

What is love?

Alex was seven years old the first time someone called her a freak.

When she's eight her best friend Sam tells her that they're still friends, but they can't be friends at school anymore. It's okay, though. She gets a library card, Sam plays with the popular girls, and on holidays and weekends they call and talk until someone's mom yells about using too many minutes.

Reading is better than going outside anyway. Going outside to play during recess means soccer balls, dodgeballs, and handballs "accidentally" flying towards her and she's not very good at dodging. Her classmates laugh when it hits her and offer to aim at her nose so she can get a free nose job; she has a bump in the middle of her nose (thanks, Dad) and they think it makes her look like a witch. At least if she's reading Ms. Gonzalez lets her stay inside, and inside there's no balls to dodge and plenty of stories to escape to.

Right now, she's really into young adult fantasy, and young adult fantasy is *really* into love triangles. Alex doesn't get the appeal because the girls in the books cry a lot, one of the guys is always a huge jerk, and the girl always ends up choosing the jerk. Sam is convinced she's in a love triangle with Stephen, who transferred last year armed with a Justin Bieber haircut and a skateboard, and Jessica, the most popular girl in fourth grade. Stephen gave Sam a pencil and didn't ask for it back, so they'll probably get married one day.

Alex gets her own first taste of a love triangle when Michael transfers into her class. Ms. Gonzalez sits him in the only empty seat, which is of course next to Alex. He's nice, sweet, and he doesn't think she's weird. He actually thinks she's kind of cool. She starts looking forward to going to school and she talks more than she has the entire school year.

… For two weeks, that is.

On the other side of Michael sits Maria, and Michael likes Maria too. Maria? Maria really likes Michael. Maria likes Michael so much, in fact, that when she notices he's talking to Alex a lot, she pulls him aside during recess and tells him all about Alex. She tells him everyone thinks Alex is weird – Alex would appreciate it if she would pass on the reason for that because she's still not sure why everyone hates her, and her mom said "they're just jealous," but her mom is her mom, so she kind of has to say that so really, please let her know – and that hanging out with Alex means you're weird too.

Nobody wants to be weird, especially not a transfer student who came in in the middle of the year. Michael stops talking to Alex. She keeps reading her books, decides love is overrated, and fourth grade really, *really* sucks. Maybe middle school will be better. Middle school has to be better.

Who loves you?

Middle school wasn't much better. High school is, somehow, worse.

Spring semester of ninth grade is mystery gum on her seat that she doesn't see until it's too late, balled up papers and pencils aimed at her head in front of teachers whose paychecks are too low to care, and whispers about the odd girl nobody likes and you shouldn't like, either. Spring semester is an introductory course to panic attacks, wet sniffles that turn into painfully dry sobs, and daily absences in the classes where it's all at its worst. Spring semester is skipping meals and working out at home, because maybe they'll like her if she's skinnier, right? Spring semester is the dean pulling her out of English class to tell her that they're considering suspension because she's truant and failing all her classes. Spring semester is a hazy walk back home, a concrete plan forming for the first time, and the blood in her veins turning to ice. Spring semester is telling her mother she swallowed a bottle of pills. Spring semester is a shell-shocked ride to the emergency room. Spring semester is *Hell*.

She wakes to quiet murmurs around her hospital bed. She isn't ready to be awake, not so soon after she tried to die, so she keeps her breathing even and her eyes shut. Not right now. She can't deal with any of this right now. Why couldn't her life work out for once. Why couldn't those pills just work?

"*Que paso*?" Her father is stricken with horror as he sits by his teenage daughter just hours after her first suicide attempt. He combs through his memory, desperate to find a warning sign, a moment he can pinpoint and say, "This, this is where I screwed up" (because he is a *machista* through and through, and the father is supposed to be the head of the household and what kind of father doesn't notice something like this?) "This is what I can fix so she never feels like this again."

She never has the heart to tell him that this wasn't the first time.

"My baby," her mother's voice is watery and weak, and even though Alex has not opened her eyes, she can see her clear as day. Brown eyes puffy and bloodshot, a lukewarm coffee clutched in her hands – brought by Alex's father, of course, when he needed to excuse himself to cry because God forbid he cries in front of the family – and her maroon acrylics peeled off after hours of compulsively biting at them. Her mother inhales but before she can form words, she's dissolved into sobs. Alex has a feeling the number of times this has happened tonight is quickly approaching double digits.

"We don't get to fall apart right now, guys," and there's her sister, her incredible sister who has always been so much stronger than Alex ever could be. "It's not about us right now. She needs us to hold it together because it's not about us, it's about her," her voice is firm, frustrated, and angry. Is she mad at Alex for not being as strong as she is, is it their parents for not realizing something was terribly wrong, is it herself for not noticing her little sister was dying, is it the world for bringing them to this point? Three different reactions, all born from fear and *love* for the girl lying on the hospital bed.

Hearing them and feeling the pain hanging in the air makes Alex feel like she's suffocating on her self-loathing. How could she do this to them? Her mother came back from a long, hard day of taking care of another person's child to find her own child desperate to die. Her father got a call during a ten-hour shift and ran so many red lights, it's a miracle he's even here and not on a hospital bed himself. Her sister is supposed to be on her college campus right now, studying, partying, *living*. She's brought them so much pain, and she didn't even have the decency to actually die. She's not only a burden but a coward, unwilling to even open her eyes to face the damage she's done.

The doctor takes that choice away from her when he walks in and announces that a nearby behavioral health center – the professional term for a psych ward –

has an opening for her. She'll be held there for the next 72 hours and released when she stops wanting to die or, more likely, when her insurance stops footing the bill. She rides an ambulance with her wrists and ankles strapped down so she can't hurt herself. It feels a bit extreme, but she did just swallow a cocktail of pills, so who says she won't try to hurl herself out of an ambulance?

She ends up staying for a week, and she'd probably stay longer if her insurance allowed it. She eats applesauce for breakfast, wears her Chucks without shoelaces, and spends half her day in group and the other half watching *Catfish* in the day room. Her roommate, Savannah, is in a perpetually bad mood thanks to detox, but she takes a liking to Alex because she only speaks when spoken to.

"So, how'd you end up here, kid?" Savannah asks her the third night. She's only 17 but she's taken to calling Alex kid, because there are practically decades between 17 and 14 when you're a teenager. By now, Alex has gotten a feel for the place. Time moves much slower here; a day feels like three back home without the noise and structure of the real world.

"I tried to kill myself," she answers quietly, because honesty is easier here. It's hard to lie to people you're in therapy with most of the day. Plus, it's not like they're in a position to judge.

"Duh. Everyone has at some point in here. But why?"

Because I'm failing all my classes and I don't know who I am if I'm not good at school. Because I ruin everything. Because nobody has liked me since elementary school and I'm starting to think it's a me problem. Because I'm built like a bridge troll. Because I'm lonely.

"I don't know," she answers instead. "It all just … became too much, I guess."

Before Savannah can answer, Amy from three doors down the hall starts to scream; she has nightmares every night, and they always come with screams. Savannah groans, stands up, marches to the door and yells into the hallway, "Will someone please just euthanize her already?!"

Before staff can yell at her, Savannah marches back to bed and puts a pillow over her head. She says nothing and Amy continues to scream while Alex loses herself in her thoughts. A few minutes later, though, Savannah calls out to her quietly.

"I get it, you know. It's hard. Life is a nightmare, and I won't lie and say it gets easier when you get older because that's bull. But look…you're a good kid. Bad people can always tell when someone's good, trust me," Savannah lets out a soft, self-deprecating laugh before continuing, "And you've got good parents, too. I've seen them coming in every day to talk and listen and *be* with you. I had those parents once, but I fucked up too many times and now? Now they just throw me in here and wait 'til the hospital kicks me to the curb, then I screw up and it happens all over again. You don't want to end up like me. Now try to sleep because Amy finally shut up, thank God, no murder charge to add to my extensive list of accomplishments."

The conversation is over, but what she said about her parents sticks with Alex. They drive thirty miles each day to visit her for thirty minutes. They bring her cookies from the gas station and talk to her about all the places they're going to take her once she's been released, the beach and botanical gardens and Porto's and anywhere that they think will help. Her mom asks her what she wants her to cook or bake for release day. Her dad tells her they can finally upgrade the computer after she begged him for months with no results. More than anything else, they tell her they love her. *They are good,* and they love her so much, more than she thinks she could ever deserve.

The months after the attempt are hard. Her secret is out in the open, and now she has a diagnosis, a therapist, and an antidepressant prescription. Her parents are on high alert for months. They hide away any non-prescribed pill or syrup she could swallow, never let her cut her own food, and they call whenever there's a moment free at work to make sure she's breathing. They ask her how she's feeling and if she hesitates for just a second too long, they grill her until they know the exact details of her day.

They all make mistakes. Her parents hover, expect her to get better faster, and don't understand that this isn't something that's going to go away just because they love her. Her sister pushes too hard, doesn't get that tough love doesn't work well on someone who hates themselves, and thinks she knows all about what Alex is going through because of a single Intro to Psych course she took in the fall. Alex keeps too much to herself because she's unaccustomed to her feelings not being a closely guarded secret. She lies to make it easier and doesn't realize that the biggest explosions come from the most bottled-up emotions.

They do their best. Her mother advocates for her to teachers and principals who have written her off as a lost cause. Her sister makes her laugh so hard she cries and there's something freeing about having tears come from joy instead of pain. Her dad doesn't comment when she emerges from her room with red eyes and an unwillingness to give anything more than monosyllabic responses, but he does bring home a dozen donuts the same day. He puts his hand on her shoulder when she's eating one at the kitchen table, and she reaches up and squeezes it so hard she thinks her fingers might break. She goes to school, takes her medication, and stays away from sharp objects and medicine cabinets

They aren't perfect. They make mistakes and they'll probably make a lot more, but no matter what happens they know they have each other. That's something worth trying for.

Do you deserve love?

It's a Wednesday night, and Alex's third weekly group therapy session just ended. She's waiting for the elevator to the first floor when she hears a voice call out to her. She turns and standing there is a beautiful brown-haired girl with red cheeks, shaking hands, and complete terror in her dark eyes. Alex smiles nervously and the girl relaxes just a bit before she takes a deep breath and blurts,
"HiI'mRoseyou'rereallyprettycanIhaveyournumber?"

Alex blinks once, twice, before weakly replying, "Sorry?" She heard her, but there's no way she heard right, right? Nobody asks her out. Nobody even looks at her. It's not real or it's some weird group therapy hazing. It has to be.

The girl's face falls briefly before she squares her shoulders and slowly repeats, "I'm Rose. I'm in your group therapy. I think you're beautiful. Can I have your number?"

Alex nods and recites it hesitantly, still not entirely certain that she hasn't broken to the point of hallucinations or that the girl isn't going to laugh in her face. Rose takes it, beams at her, and walks back to the waiting room where her friends are anxiously waiting. Alex walks into the elevator and thinks that she hears squealing as the door closes.

Rose invites her to the movies a few days later. Alex isn't sure if it's a date until she's being handed a box of chocolates and a teddy bear, and even then, it could technically still be hazing. They watch a terrible movie based off Alex's favorite book series, *Vampire Academy*, and she swears up and down to Rose that the books are much better than the nightmare they just watched and apologizes profusely for subjecting her to a two-hour train wreck. Rose kisses her for the first time as the sun starts to set and okay, maybe this is a real date.

She tells her parents that she's dating a girl that same week. She clarifies that this does not make her a lesbian – there's a few cute male actors in there and maybe like, one classmate – but that sexuality is fluid and really, you never know. The last year has been all about rolling with the punches for Alex and her family, so they take it in stride despite years of devout Catholicism. They aren't thrilled but they make it a point to loudly denounce homophobia whenever the topic comes up and honestly, that's enough for her.

Rose lives in a predominantly white suburban neighborhood that's very, very far from Alex. Every time Alex visits, she marvels at the concept of not locking your doors, being able to go outside alone past 6pm, and having actual relationships with your neighbors. They go to Easter egg hunts, have awkward family dinners at Souplantation, and steal kisses at Rose's sweet 16. They say I love you too fast, as all teenagers do, and they act as though this will last forever.

It doesn't, though, and Alex gets to experience her first heartbreak. She stuffs her face with donuts and swears that she will never love again. She cries to a frankly embarrassing amount of Adele and writes terrible poetry until even she's sick of herself. She imagines her future filled entirely with cats, and then she remembers she's allergic and likes dogs more anyway. Same point, though.

Thankfully, her head clears enough for her to scrub all traces of her poems from the Earth, because nobody deserves to be subjected to heartbroken teenager poetry. She still wants the future with the dogs, but preferably without the crippling loneliness. She decides she'd rather chop her ears off than hear *Someone Like You* one more time, so she takes the album off her iPod. It's closure.

When a boy with the kindest eyes she's ever seen and a blinding smile wants to know her, her first thought is of Rose. She thinks of the way they made each other laugh, the clumsy kisses whenever they had a moment alone, the glow in her heart, and the way love slowly went cold when things started falling apart. She thinks of having it again, and again, and again until one day it doesn't go cold and instead continues to glow. So, she smiles, and lets herself try.

Is love all you need?

They're fighting again. Of course, they're fighting again.

It wasn't always like this. That's always the story though, isn't it? It's good, it's everything, then something happens, or someone changes, and everything turns to … this. Missed calls, cancelled dates, messages unanswered for days, and them, fighting again.

Every day that she loves him is a decision to swallow poison. Acid eats at her heart and still she keeps drinking, because she'd rather choke on love than face a world without it. Her love is tinged with desperation now because she's known a world without him and it's dark and lonely and how is she supposed to let this go?

She remembers the way her heart glowed with the people before him. Funny how that glow that had once seemed all-consuming now pales in the face of a love that feels like the sun. They all wanted her to change in some way or another, but he had taken her as she was, and he had loved her so much it was borderline suffocating. The things she would give to feel suffocated right now.

It would be easier if she knew there was no way they could work. It would be easier if he stopped making her laugh, if she didn't know him better than anyone else, or if they didn't agree on the vision of a yellow house filled with light and laughter. At least then there'd be an obstacle or roadblock they could tackle, and they could change it, destroy it, or agree it was too much to overcome. They could stay together or separate knowing that they had done all they could, even if all they could would never be enough.

A younger her scoffed at characters in movies, TV shows, and books that left the person they loved because "it wasn't the right time." If that's the love of your life, you make it the right time. You grow together, you hold on, you don't let go because letting go means giving up and what kind of love is that? If she ever met someone who her heart recognized as the one all the love songs were written about, she'd never let anything take that from her.

Then she found it, and now it's halfway out the door because it isn't the right time. Her life is falling apart right before her eyes and this is one of the last pieces to give. If anything, she feels ridiculous for even worrying about this right now when there are bigger, uglier monsters out to get her. A distant part of her, the part that has actually paid attention during all the therapy she's done in the last few years, knows that it's easier for her to focus on the petty pain of a break-up than on the nuclear bomb of pain that's rapidly hurtling towards her.

She could think about her mom's deportation to El Salvador and how there's a chance they'll keep her there instead of letting her come back, but it hurts less to think about the way he used to look at her. She could replay the conversation with her principal when he told her she had 60 credits standing between her and a piece of paper that meant the last four years were worth it, she could think about the fact that her classmates have college acceptances and prom night after four years of copying each other's homework, or she could replay their first date and think about how they already had their last one without even knowing it.

She could think of what she has, her ever-present demons. They tell her not to eat and tell her to eat everything in the same breath. When she waits for the train, they fill her ears with a buzzing, and she thinks about jumping more than she'd like to admit. They repeat the cruel taunts and whispers from people with a preconceived idea of a girl they never bothered to know. They make her hands shake and her chest feel like it's caving in every time she enters a school. They have her sneaking cigarettes with her classmates at continuation school and chugging cough syrup like it's orange juice. Alternatively, she could think about what she's about to lose: him.

The pain of losing him is masking the pain of losing *everything*, and a part of her is grateful for that. Pain is pain, though, and if there was anything she could do to stop their march to the executioner's block she would. She knows she can't, and even if she could she shouldn't. She can't stop a yellow house from burning down when she's on fire too.

At any other time, could they survive this? Neither could answer that, but she knows if that time does exist, it isn't now. But *God,* does she wish it was now. She loves him so much that she doesn't think she'll ever love anyone like that again, and maybe she doesn't want to because this, this burns. What does she know, though? For all she knows, in five years he's a distant memory buried underneath hundreds of happier days. Twenty years and it's a story she tells her children when they come home crying about the person they think is their greatest love. Maybe she doesn't need a love like the sun. Maybe she should pay attention to the nuclear bomb instead.

That fight isn't the end of them and neither are the fights after it. The end is much quieter, more turning off the machines than a knife in the chest. He tells her what she already knows, he's leaving but she's still a wonderful person, just not the person for him. She lets him go quietly. No fights. She can't fight this anymore.

Who is the love of your life?
She can, however, fight herself.

Her mother comes back, this time with a green card so they never experience that nightmare again. She doesn't graduate, but on the day she gets her GED she dances on a train platform in Downtown LA and it feels just as good. She goes to group therapy every week, individual therapy twice a month, stops the medication because, apparently, she should've paid attention to the "worsening depression" side effect, and replaces codeine with chamomile. California changes the smoking law to 21 as she's going through nicotine withdrawal, and she could've possibly passed for 18 to a skeevy liquor store cashier who only cared about how low-cut her top was, but nobody with semi-functioning eyesight would believe she's 21. She could go for the sketchy places her classmates would whisper about, but hey, she'll take it as a sign.

Alex starts summer classes eight months after dropping out. The first time she sees a former classmate she has a panic attack so violent that she ends up dry heaving in the bathroom. By the end of that semester, it's gone down to heart palpitations and shaking hands. Two years in and the first week of every semester after is a pit of anxiety in her stomach each time she walks into a new classroom, but one week out of sixteen isn't so bad.

The first time she gets an A, she buys herself a $6 coffee from the cafe near school and cries on her walk home. Maybe some of the tears are for the expensive coffee but most of them are for her, for the girl who cried and screamed in her father's car when her principal looked at her like she was nothing but a disappointment, for the girl who spent the last year of her life stitching together a reason to keep going. The tenth time and she's vindicated, solid proof in her hands that she was not wasted potential solely because she never received a singular piece of paper. Maybe it's unhealthy to get that much validation out of a grade, but everyone needs to get their ego boosted from somewhere. She's still a work in progress, and that's okay.

Every now and then, she even considers dating again. The first time someone asks her out, she shuts down completely and goes out with him only in the sense that her physical body is there. Every time he tries to talk to her, she smiles blandly and gives monosyllabic replies until he stops trying. He touches her and she flinches away. Shockingly, there isn't a second date. That's okay, too.

There are a few others after, like the guy who decides to tell her halfway through a slice of pizza that he's a sex addict. Alex is all about oversharing so this doesn't faze her much, at least not until they're halfway back to campus, and he tells her that "the bathroom in the Chemistry building is pretty empty around this time of day, how much time do you have before class?"

So maybe there's not many winners in her dating life, but at least the idea of a dating life doesn't make her want to lock herself in her room and cry to Taylor Swift for hours anymore. Sure, she spent a frankly shameful amount of time doing exactly that (if it's a break-up song, she's probably heard of it) and writing her trademark terrible poetry about what shade of blue his eyes were (somewhere around #B4D8E7), but it's been three years now and she only does that on anniversaries. Kidding! But not really. It's still progress, give her a break.

It's messy. Her friends move away for college and with college comes new friends, new boyfriends, girlfriends, and drifting apart. She makes new ones and it's not the same, but she's also been friends with the same people since middle school, so maybe this is just the universe telling her to get out more. She's in terrible physical health – cycling between starving and bingeing isn't kind to your metabolism, and she hasn't voluntarily run since a knee surgery when she was 14 – so she makes herself learn to cook food with actual nutrients and starts going to the gym. It turns out that exercise actually *does* release endorphins and hey, she can even open jars herself now. She dyes her hair bright green – a childhood dream Sam talked her out of because she said she would look like an Oompa Loompa – and on her walk back from the salon, a woman who reeks of tequila, even though it's 2pm, shouts that she looks like a clown. Alex has never loved her appearance more.

There are bad days. She wakes up and everything in her is off-balance, her smile is slightly plastic, and there's shadows dancing in the corners of her vision. Some days school gets overwhelming and she thinks about dropping all of her classes to become a dancing mascot on Hollywood Boulevard. She deals with it by jumping on a bus to the beach, staying home and napping with her dog, or paying way too much for a pint of vegan ice cream because she's a responsible adult who respects her lactose intolerance; sometimes, she has to do all three and throws in a donut, too. The world doesn't stop and the next day, she's ready to keep going too.

She isn't lonely when she's alone because, my god, does she have love. She has her family, friends, and now, she even has a dog. Is there any love truer and more unconditional than the love of a pet? Granted his love for her is probably based off how many treats she gives him every week, but is that really so different than most human relationships?

And, of course, Alex has Alex. She buys herself hair dye and overpriced artisanal ice cream, swallows enough melatonin to get to bed before the sunrise, and drags herself to school, the gym, and whatever trendy dessert place she finds on Yelp. She cries, laughs, lives, and she wakes up every morning to do it all over again. She's powered by love and it's all her own, stitched together from the love she has and hasn't had, sure, but still her own.

Autumn Spectacular Journey to Golden Park
by Vasyl Flotski

During my school years, like all other children, I had many school excursions, but this excursion was special, dizzying, like in the movies. This is an exciting story in which there were betrayals, fighting, and love. And now I will try to tell you all this.

It all started with the fact that my teacher, Mr. Prokopenko, offered to organize a trip to the famous Ukrainian park, "National Dendrological Park Sofievsky." In the autumn, this park turned into a fabulous place with thousands of shades of brown and gold leaves. And very often people called it Golden Park. Since it was just in the middle of autumn, Mr. Prokopenko very quickly organized a tour.

Early Friday morning, my parents brought me to the backyard of the school, where our trip was to begin. This morning was chilly, with a drizzling rain, and in this weather, I did not want to go anywhere, but it was too late to retreat. Moreover, my parents quickly wished me good luck and fun, and immediately left. Mr. Prokopenko took about 15 minutes to gather all the children and strictly assigned us our seats on the bus. I got a place near the aisle, not the best place for a long trip. At 6:00 AM, the bus started, and my journey began.

The bus was cold and smelled like forgotten food. *There's definitely no one who had ever cleaned this bus,* I thought. To make matters worse, in the front of the bus was a guy who wanted to vomit all the way. Toward the middle of the bus ride, he totally brought his breakfast back up. It was a terrible four hours in my life. However, this smelly way led to one of the most beautiful places in Ukraine.

At about 10 AM, we arrived at Golden Park. Since this was my first trip to this park, I did not know what to expect. My first impression was that it was a terrible place. Just imagine a small parking lot with a bunch of buses and a long, old stone wall, beyond which nothing could be seen. *Where is Golden Park?* I wondered. However, my disappointment did not last long. After 15 minutes, we were following Mr. Prokopenko through the main gate and immediately in front of us spread out an unlimited park, with countless trees. The sun's rays filled all these trees and their yellow and brown leaves shimmered in the rays of the sun. It really did seem that everything sparkled like gold. Suddenly, I understood why this park was called Golden.

The park's insane beauty and indescribable views were interrupted by our guide, who began to show us different types of trees that had been growing there a very long time. In fact, many of them were listed in the *Red Book,* a book of endangered plants and animals. This boring tour guide also talked about how important it was to love nature and *blah blah blah.* For a ten-year-old boy, this was absolutely useless information. For five hours we wandered through the park with this guide until finally it was time for us students to have free movement in the park.

Mr. Prokopenko divided us into small groups of 6 to 8 people and allowed us to explore the park on our own, with one condition: "Do not, under any circumstances, leave the park's territory." I volunteered to be the head of our group, but Mr. Prokopenko stopped me. He appointed as our leader the main teenager, a 13-year-old boy. It was not fair, since I felt much smarter.

This teenager named Anton started to make himself a great boss, and he told us what we should do and where we should go. But I was not going to tolerate it. I had a secret hidden in my backpack. It was a map that my father had given me in secret, with the words, "If possible, be sure to look at these places that I marked on the map."

I want to clarify. When I was ten years old, there were no smartphones, no Internet, and no GPS. The map of the park was not sold at the entrance. It could only be bought in a town nearby, about 20 minutes away. So, my map, with its secret notes from my father, was worth its weight in gold.

As we walked along, I persuaded several of my friends to escape from the tyranny of our 13-year-old boss. And they seemed to agree with my plan, but suddenly they betrayed me. One of my friends told Anton that I was staging a revolt, planning an escape. Anton was very angry hearing it. He came right up to me and hit me very hard in the stomach. It was painful, and even more painful because my friends had betrayed me. After a long moment, I got up, wiped away the tears, and pulled myself together. I made a decision. It was necessary to escape on my own and explore the park alone.

Since it was about an hour before sunset, I decided not to postpone the escape, and right away I disappeared. I jumped into the nearby bushes, and there I began to move through dense thickets of plants. I believed that Anton would not rush to run after me into the bushes; besides, he would hardly have left the other children by themselves. And that's how it happened, so my plan worked.

For a while, I still ran in a panic and was afraid that he would catch me and beat me again. But soon I stopped and calmed down. Catching my breath, I took out the map in order to understand where I was. My father had taught me how to determine the directions of the world, and I could navigate quite well. Choosing a direction to the west, I set off towards a hill. When I climbed the hill, I saw houses and part of a monument in the distance, and I immediately knew where I was. Looking at the map, I chose the place closest to me that my father had marked, and I went in that direction. The walk took about ten minutes. It was another hill with trees and thick grass. When I climbed it, I finally understood why my father had marked this place on the map. I had a wonderful view of almost the entire park. I saw a beautiful blue pond, and yellow-purple fields with flowers, and wide trees with golden leaves. Moreover, I saw in the distance a square in a nearby town where people met. They looked like little ants. It was a divine beauty.

The sun went down, and the beauty went out. I had to move back to my group. After all, everyone probably thought I was lost. After half an hour or so, I climbed onto an asphalt road that led me to the people. Soon, I found one of the park guards who escorted me to my group. But to my surprise, no one was looking for me. As it turned out, Anton simply did not tell anyone about me, and he intimidated the other children who were in our group so that they remained silent.

When Anton saw me, he ran up to me and began to scream and intimidate me. I did not understand what he was talking about, and I tried to escape from him. But I failed, and he hit me again. This time, I decided to fight back. It was my mistake because we were not equal weight, so it was really an unequal fight. He was definitely stronger and significantly taller than I was. A few blows and he knocked me to the ground, ripped my jacket and smashed my elbow to blood. But a miracle saved me from this monster. A girl ran up to our fight, and she started beating Anton with her backpack. Anton quickly left me alone and ran away.

My rescuer was named Nastya. She was definitely older than I was. She had blonde hair and green eyes. As she helped me up, she spoke to me. We began to talk and did not notice that one hour passed. By this time all of us began to be called to our buses. As it turned out, Nastya was from another school in a different city. So, for me, it meant that I would not see her again. Realizing that, I was sad. Just before the bus left, unexpectedly, she kissed me. It was my first kiss. I still remember that she smelled of bubblegum. We took different buses and after a while I rode home.

So ended my amazing and very eventful journey, which included a nauseous bus ride, an absolutely boring excursion through a beautiful park, the betrayal of friends, an escape from a teenaged tyrant, an unforgettable sunset that will remain in my memory for a lifetime, an unequal fight, a miraculous salvation and, most importantly, love. Truly I have not forgotten this magical park.

Silence in the Crowd (A True Story)
by S M Keramat Ali

It was December 15, 1992 at noon when I was cooking fish after coming from college, but I became absent-minded and the fish became overly burned and unsuitable to eat. I tried to do the same thing three times repeatedly, but each time the same thing happened. I felt restless in my mind though I could not find a reason. However, I completed lunch because I was hungry. After half an hour, my neighbor notified me that I received a phone call because I had no cell phone or land phone. The news came to me like a bolt out of the blue because it was the news of my beloved mom's stroke. I was at a loss about what to do. I understood why I burned the fish repeatedly; it was about the close connection of a mother with her child.

I was staying in the capital city in an apartment to study while my parents were living in a rural area. Usually I needed about ten to twelve hours to reach my village home. Without any delay, I started for home. I reached the station in the afternoon and got onto a bus. While the bus was moving, I could visualize my mom's smiley face when I returned home and her gloomy face when I would have to leave the house. I heard from people that my mom prayed to God and said, "Oh God, gift me a son whether he is black or lame or blind. I want to hear a sound 'Ma' from a son." I like to add that I was born after five sisters, and there was a tradition in rural Bangladesh that a son would bear the ancestors family line. If there was no son, then the father married again for a son. I indirectly brought peace to our family. My mother loved me very much, but she never hesitated for a moment to send me to the capital city for a better education.

The bus was moving fast and crossing village after village. Cold air was touching me. After four hours, the bus reached a river where it had to cross by ferry. People were buying some snacks and ate them. I attempted to buy some snacks with the money that Mom gave me as pocket money. My father didn't know it. Anyway, my mind did not allow me to buy food. In the meantime, the ferry started moving to cross the River Padma. I was watching the large waves, going up and down, which reminded me of the economy of our family. My father was an elementary teacher as well as a farmer. But during the flood of 1991, our crops were damaged, and we had to struggle very much. Consequently, my parents could not send money for my education. At that time, to manage my tuition fees, I earned some money as a private tutor by teaching young students. One time, before going to spend vacation with my parents, I bought some clothes for my father and mother. Once I bought a pair of shoes for my mom, but she kept the shoes inside the closet and told others that, if she wore the shoes and walked, her son would be hurt. The pair of shoes is still new in her closet.

After crossing the river, the bus started moving again. My tension was increasing because I did not know about the condition of my mother. About 2am, I got off the bus and approached our house situated by the highway. Everything about the house was as usual. The outside light was on. I knocked on the door, and my father opened the door. Some of our relatives and well-wishers were still in our house. As soon as I went to the bed where my ailing mom was lying, she tried to call my name, but she could only mumble. Tears were rolling down from her eyes. She was only trying to keep me in her heart. After seeing my mom, I felt relaxed. After some time, I went to the nearby clinic for an ambulance to take my mom to a good hospital, but the driver was not available. I waited for him until 9am and managed to take my mom to the Medical College Hospital at about 12pm.

After doing all the formalities, my mom was admitted, and doctors started to give her treatment. Initially, doctors tried to diagnose the disease by doing some tests. I was very optimistic that my mom would recover from her illness. Senior doctors made a medical plan to ensure better treatment. They were using different medical instruments for improving the condition of my mom. In the evening, the senior doctors went away. Before going away, they gave the visiting doctors and the nurses some instructions to follow through the night. All the medicines and injections were not available in the hospital. So, I was busy supplying them by buying them from an outside medical store. At midnight, it was becoming difficult for my mom to breathe easily because her cough was growing worse. The nurses became tired, so I learned from them how to operate the machine to clear her mouth. Sometimes her hands and legs were bending and were becoming cold. At that time, I massaged her so that her legs and hands would become normal. My attention was on how to save my mom from this critical condition. I wanted to hear a word from my mom. Instead, what I saw were tears in her eyes.

In the morning, our relatives, friends and well-wishers gathered in the hospital. I felt very happy to see them, and my energy increased. At about 9am, I was more hopeful to see the senior doctors. They instructed the visitors to stay away from the patient. They observed my mom, and all the records of the night. At one stage, they called me to buy an injection from the nearby medical store. When I was rushing out, I met our well-wishers in the corridor of the hospital. I had no time to spare for them. After buying the injection, I was rushing back again. To my surprise, I found no well-wishers in the corridor. I heard no sounds or no discussions. I approached the inside of the hospital room. All the visitors and doctors encircled the bed where my mom was lying. The whole sky was about to break down over my head. As I stepped over to her bed, I felt as if I was about to collapse. Everyone was staring at me and the injection in my hand. What I found was silence in the crowd, and my mom was covered with a white sheet of cloth. She had no pain, no breathing problems and no worries about me.

For German Alberto Cruz Lopez
by Kenny Carranza

It was sometime around 3:15 in the morning and
sweltering
in our room,

when I imagined the helicopter blades
replaced
our sputtering ceiling fan.

The next morning, I read why
divers were in the lake.

It took hours,
upon hours,
upon hours
to find the body, but
they found him.

I didn't know the
young man; but

now,
as I look at the lake,

I see floating swans,
forever frozen in time at
their funeral procession.

The lotus flowers evolved
from a symbol of
immortality,
into a fragrant

eviction notice,
clumsily taped to a
wrought iron
door,
informing everybody
that it is time
to move

on.

Procession for the Birth of the Dying
by Daniel Renteria

Sophia in love with the snake.

There, the man - he is dead.

The emptiness of the room quenched with blood.

The stain slowly spreads inviting the thirsty tongues of

    beasts and holy creatures,

Angels who desire flesh; the temptation of mortality and

    its virtues; of the infinite transformation.

A mirror and a vision:

Surrounded by prayer, as if in a Mexican altar;

Elderly women deeply sobbing, healing the internal

    wounds of sin - facing their mortality.

Their words speak to the flesh, they taste the face of

    God.

They have done it again and again. It is all too familiar

    like the smell of flowers.

It's cold here, I thirst for the warmth of the flames,

The candles slowly melting into the corneas of my eyes.

I am there, whole, nestled against the reality of life and

    insatiable binding of death.

    Into the sanctuary, into the senseless asylum.

      I await the sunrise.

The dormant breath.

Gently rise.

Funeral.

Awakening.

Habits
by Yahaira Avila

Our plans? Discarded.

Along with your vows.

The words expressed by you both,

Like knife.

The same one used to cut the tension in our home.

But this isn't our home, not anymore.

The lights in here are gaslights, the emotions in here are

overreactions.

The tones, condescending as not to break me.

But I have slowly been breaking for weeks now.

Now it's just physically manifested.

Your words, cunning and deep, your actions

Shallow, self-serving.

Conveniently, you claimed toxicity.

Yet, this is not the first time we have walked this road.

Ever the creatures of habit.

Think Outside the Box
by William Morales

I suggest you pay attention, I'm about to drop
some knowledge
Something that they won't ever dare teach in college
So break it down real good, take it all and roll it
Take a hit of my thoughts and let your brain absorb this
I wish you would get a vision that would let you envision
the world through my eyes
And see what I have seen as time flies by
You would have to buckle up, hold on tight
and try not to blink
'Cause the world through my perspective
can really make you think
I see the fears of the fearless
And the flaws of the flawless
I've seen winners have losses
And the brawls of the drawless
See, this world will have you
Pondering why
Why all the honest people in the world
Are living up such a lie?
Tell me, what would you do
If every single lie you've ever heard happened to be true?
And everyone you encounter sits behind the counter
and never gives you a break
Tell me how much more could you take
When all they do is take
Every right a mistake
Real friends turn fake
Reputations at stake
Relationships break
Temptation a snake

Every day a new ache
Every time you awake
Everything starts to shake
It's all a huge quake
Slow down hit the brakes
This is my life, take a flip through the pages
I have a tale to be told through the ages
And then maybe you'll understand all my rages
How it feels that through all our lives
We've been living in cages
Isn't it outrageous?
Regrets left behind in all our life stages
Fighting all week to keep our minimum wages
But we never stop to think
And never think to stop
Keep running like the faucet in the kitchen sink
Always leaking that one drop
Did I lose you in my thoughts or are you right behind?
Take a good look around and thank God you aren't blind
Appreciate the small things and those around you
Don't let anyone influence or misguide you
Just think of all the innocent people doing time
Wrapped up in a case and sentenced for a crime
Doing time for a crime that they didn't commit
I mean what more can they do than just wait and sit?
So don't let an opportunity pass you by
That feels almost as bad as seeing your mama cry
So stop a few seconds and envision the world
through your own vision
Open up your mind to the perspective and the transition
Train your untrained eye
And don't fill your mind with dirt and rocks
So that every moment that passes by
You can think outside the box...

And We Wonder
by Jesmin Sultana

When time seems to pass by,
We wonder…
When it moves slow,
We wonder…

When we are flooded with joy,
We wonder…
When we are drowned in grief,
We wonder…

Wondering only has boundaries,
As long as our experiences.
The more we have,
The more it becomes dense.

It is never decided what we will wonder,
It is that particular moment that triggers it.
And at that particular moment, as time freezes,
We detail our wonder every bit.

It seems that the sounds are fading,
The voices inside rising.
It tells us something,
We just have to understand the real meaning.

One deep breath,
And everything becomes clear.
One long blink,
As we wonder…

Special Thanks:

Los Angeles City College Administration

Dr. Mary P Gallagher, *President*

Dr. James Lancaster, *VP of Academic Affairs*

Mr. James Reeves, *VP of Administrative Services*

Dr. Regina Smith, *VP of Student Services*

Dr. Themla Day, Dr. Carol Kozeracki, Dr. Vi Ly, Ms. Angelica Ramirez, Ms. Fabiola Mora, Dr. Armando Figueroa-Rivera, Dr. Imelda Perez: *Deans of Academic Affairs*

Mr. Alen Andriassian, Dr. Jeremy Villar, Dr. Drew Yamanishi, Mr. Jeffrey Holmes: *Deans of Student Services*

Dr. Anna Badalyan, *Dean of Institutional Effectiveness*

The faculty of the English/ESL Department of Los Angeles City College

Helen Khachatryan, *LACC Foundation*

Robert Schwartz, *LACC Foundation*

Alexandra Wiesenfeld, C*hair of Visual and Media Arts*

Marlene McCurtis and Susie Tanner, *TheatreWorkers Project*

Made in the USA
Las Vegas, NV
24 October 2022

58062147R00076